At the
Edge of
the
Night

FRIEDO LAMPE

At the Edge of the Night

Translated from
the German
by Simon Beattie

HESPERUS

Published by Hesperus Press Limited
28 Mortimer Street, London W1W 7RD
www.hesperuspress.com

First Published in German in 1933
This translation first published by Hesperus Press Limited, 2019
From the 1999 German edition:
Friedo Lampe, Am Rande der Nacht
Roman
Mit einem Nachwort hg. von Johannes Graf
Wallstein Verlag, Göttingen 1999

Introduction and English Language translation by Simon Beattie 2019

Edited by Linden Lawson
Typeset by Madeline Meckiffe
Printed in Barcelona, Spain by Liber Duplex

ISBN 9781843916543

For Jackie Brooker and
the late Andrew Ormanroyd,
who set me on the path.

SB

TRANSLATOR'S INTRODUCTION

'I never have any luck with my books,' commented Friedo Lampe in 1944, after an air raid destroyed almost the entire edition of his latest book, a collection of short stories. Just over ten years before, his first, the novel *Am Rande der Nacht* ('At the Edge of the Night'), had been banned by the Nazis. Lampe had spent a life in books—as reader, collector, librarian, editor and writer—but it was a life of struggles and setbacks that ultimately ended in tragedy.

Lampe was born on 4 December 1899, in the north German city of Bremen, a place which would exert a particular influence on his writing and serve as the setting for his first book. At the age of five he was diagnosed with bone tuberculosis in his left ankle and sent to a children's clinic over 100 miles away, on the East Frisian island of Nordeney; he spent a total of three years there, away from his family, before being pronounced cured, but it left him disabled for the rest of his life. As a teenager Lampe was a voracious reader—he devoured Hoffmann, Kleist, Büchner, Rilke, Mann and Kafka, but also Boccaccio, Cervantes, Dostoevsky, Shakespeare, Dickens and Poe—and an insatiable book buyer: 'It really is an illness with me. I just have to buy every book, even if I don't have the money.' After the First World War, during which he was given a desk job with the mess sergeant at a local barracks, Lampe studied literature, art history and philosophy at Heidelberg (with Friedrich Gundolf and Karl Jaspers), Munich, and Freiburg (with Edmund Husserl), before returning to Bremen and work, first as a trainee at, but soon sub- then associate editor of the family magazine *Schünemanns Monatshefte*. In 1931 the magazine ceased publication (a victim of the Great Depression), and Lampe retrained as a librarian; he soon found work with the public libraries in Hamburg, where he was responsible for acquisitions.

It was in Hamburg that he became acquainted with young writers such as Wilhelm Emanuel Süskind (father of Patrick) and Joachim Maass, who wrote for the avant-garde monthly arts magazine *Der Kreis*. The Nazis' seizure of power in January 1933 soon put paid to the magazine, which was shut down months later. Many of Lampe's writer friends went into exile.

But Lampe himself was writing, and *Am Rande der Nacht* was published by Rowohlt in Berlin at the end of October 1933. The title page of the first edition is actually dated 1934, but by then the book was already unavailable: in December 1933 it was seized by the Nazis, withdrawn from sale, and later included on their official 'list of damaging and undesirable writings' due to its homoerotic content and depiction of an interracial liaison between a black man and a German woman. Lampe wrote at the time that the book was born into a regime where it was unable to breathe, but hoped that one day it might rise again.

Am Rande der Nacht is not simply a rare example of a novel by a gay German writer in the Thirties. It is also an early work of magic realism—'The way spaces, periods of time, slide into each other, something which is sometimes called surrealism, is an artistic method Lampe liked to employ,' wrote the author Kurt Kusenberg. 'People live their lives as if a dream'—and exhibits a new narrative form which, in Germany at least, was largely without precedent. It has no one main character, but rather weaves together the actions of various people on one September evening. Rowohlt's chief editor at the time, Paul Meyer, wrote: 'The novel is good, stylistically. It is not always easy to read because, like the novels of Dos Passos, it doesn't have a continuous plot, but a sequence of quick-changing, parallel scenes.' The book's dust jacket, when Rowohlt published it, drew attention to this. In large letters across the front cover it stated: 'A remarkable novel. Novel? A stream of images and scenes, with many characters: children, old people and young people, men and women, townsfolk, performers, students and seamen. Things happen as they happen, horrible things, touching things, exciting, gentle, all against the backdrop and in the atmosphere of a sultry summer night on the waterfront of a north German city. A melancholy, beautiful book, akin to the timeless writing of Hofmannsthal, Eduard Keyserling and Herman Bang'. (The dust jacket advertised other Rowohlt publications which were also subsequently banned by the Nazis: Musil's *Der Mann ohne Eigenschaften* and *In einem andern Land*, the 1930 translation of Hemingway's *A Farewell to Arms*.)

Lampe loved ancient Greek literature; his later heroes were Kleist, Otto Ludwig and Cervantes. But it was his keen interest in the cinema which influenced his first book most. Lampe conceived the novel as *filmartig* ('film-like', 'cinematic') when he was writing it, intending 'everything [to be] light and fluid, only loosely connected, graphic, lyrical, full of atmosphere'. Writing in 1959, Heinz Piontek called Lampe 'one of the first German writers to transfer the technology of film onto prose. His eye has something of a camera about it, dissecting the action into "sequences"'; the editors of Rowohlt's 1986 collected edition drew attention to Lampe's 'soft cross-fades, clean cuts or deftly executed pan shots.' As Lampe wrote in 'Laterna magica', a short story published only after his death: 'The most important thing is the cut.'

Nazi censorship policies also made things difficult for Lampe as a book-buying librarian, and in 1937 he moved to Berlin, where he accepted a job as an editor with Rowohlt. Lampe's second novel, *Septembergewitter* ('September Storm'), came out in December that year but sales were poor, in part due to bad timing: it was too close to Christmas, and by January 1938 the new book was old news.

Lampe carried on at Rowohlt until the end of September 1939—the press was shut down by the Nazis, and Ernst Rowohlt himself left Germany—when he worked as an editor first for Goverts, at the time one of the leading literary publishers in the country, then, from July 1940 onwards, for the recently founded Karl Heinz Henssel Verlag. In 1943–4 he edited a series of works by eighteenth- and nineteenth-century German authors for Diederichs in Jena. During the war Lampe produced very little of his own work, only a dozen short stories. He was gripped by fear: fear that friends, or he himself (though his disability apparently saved him from this), would be called up for military service, fear of not having enough to eat, fear of losing his friends, job and home, fear of being arrested for his homosexuality, fear that a long-desired volume of his own collected works would never appear. And his fears proved true: nearly all his friends were called up; then, in the night of 22–3 November 1943, his flat was completely destroyed in an air raid on Berlin. Lampe was beside himself, and reports in letters that only a couple of pieces of furniture could be saved. His greatest loss was his books: 'That's the worst thing. I've spent my whole life building up that library. It was unique, in its way: a comprehensive collection of German literature from its beginnings to the present. And the best translations of foreign literature, all systematically collected and arranged, some in valuable editions'.

A new edition of *Septembergewitter* (printed in a collection of short stories entitled *Von Tür zu Tür*, 'From Door to Door', in which any English names in the novel were replaced with Danish ones) was planned for 1944, but it was beset with problems: the threat of closure for Goverts Verlag, a lack of paper for printing. Finally, paper was secured and the type set, only for most of the edition to go up in flames during an air raid on Leipzig.

After the destruction of his flat Lampe had moved to Kleinmachnow, between Berlin and Potsdam, where he was given refuge by the writer Ilse Molzahn, whom he had got to know when working at Rowohlt. She had left the city for the relative safety of Silesia, and was only too pleased to know someone would be living in her house. Lampe found living there an 'idyll' after the horrors of Berlin.

By the end of 1944, Lampe had been drafted into working for a branch of the Nazi Foreign Office, editing reports from intercepted enemy news broadcasts. As the months went by he understood all too clearly the course the war was taking, the regime's impending defeat and the nature of its crimes. Lampe called the work 'gruelling, a real grind. Six hours a day of stressful, eye-straining proof work, lots of night shifts, constant tiredness... But I am lucky with how things are. I was examined again recently and marked down as "out of commission".'

The war had taken its toll. Lampe, who was a big man and known for his healthy appetite, had by 1942 already lost a lot of weight. Three years later and he was, by all accounts, a shadow of his former physical self. In the spring of 1945, Molzahn returned with her family to Kleinmachnow. With Soviet forces moving into neighbouring Wannsee, she wanted to press on to Nauen which, it was rumoured, had been taken by American troops. She urged Lampe to go with them but he instead returned to Kleinmachnow, where he was later stopped by two Red Army soldiers who demanded his papers. Lampe, dressed in a dark-blue coat, hat, and with a rucksack on his back, did as he was asked. But something was not quite right. The Russians began to question him, as they did not believe that the man standing before them and the man in the photograph were one and the same. Due to the privations of war, and gnawed by constant fear, Lampe had lost so much weight that he no longer resembled the photograph on his identity card. After five minutes of trying to make himself intelligible to the soldiers, Lampe was ordered onto a nearby patch of grass. He raised his arm across his face when two shots were fired, and he fell to the ground. The date was 2 May 1945, just six days before the end of the war.

Lampe's body was taken to a local Catholic priest and interred in a nearby cemetery. His grave is marked by a simple wooden cross, carved with the words 'Du bist nicht einsam': 'You are not alone'.

Hermann Hesse later wrote: 'His novel *Am Rande der Nacht* appeared in 1933. I read it at the time with great interest, as German prose writers of such quality were rare even then... And what struck us at the time... as so beautiful and powerful has not paled, it has withstood; it proves itself with the best, and captivates and delights just as then.'

A Note on the Text

Am Rande der Nacht was first published in 1933, when it was banned by the Nazis. Rowohlt published a new version of the novel, with the 'offensive' passages removed, in 1949 under the title *Ratten und Schwäne* ('Rats and Swans'). This expurgated text was reprinted in subsequent German editions (i.e. the two collected editions of Lampe's works, 1955 and 1986) and served as the source text for both the French (1970) and Dutch (1974) translations of the novel. A new edition, complete and unexpurgated, following the text of the first edition, was published in 1999 to mark the centenary of Lampe's birth. This is the text I have followed here.

In his haunting book *Dora Bruder* (also known as *The Search Warrant* in English), Patrick Modiano devotes a two-page digression to Lampe and his novel. He cannot fathom exactly what the Nazis objected to, but the translation he had read was based on an expurgated version of the text.

Lampe's original manuscript of *Am Rande der Nacht* is held at the Deutsches Literaturarchiv in Marbach (call number 88.43.3). Interestingly, it is not the final version of the novel, as printed in 1933. He must have subsequently altered certain passages, and made further cuts, before publication.

Simon Beattie
Buckinghamshire, June 2018

FRIEDO LAMPE

At the
Edge of
the
Night

Destinies many weave with mine,
All intermingled by life.
Hugo von Hofmannsthal

Hans was getting tired of waiting. 'This is ridiculous,' he said. 'If they don't come soon, I'm off. My legs ache, my eyes ache... We've been crouched here, looking, for ages.'

'They'll come in a minute. You'll see,' said Erich, but he sounded less optimistic. 'It's just got to get a bit darker.'

'Yes, so dark that you can't see anything, and then you'll say: there they are, and it'll be a root. We know you. Daft. Just showing off,' snorted Hans, as he watched two swans, their necks proud, swim silently across the middle of the moat. They were heading for their little house. Hans clicked his tongue, but their heads did not turn, not even slightly.

'They came yesterday. Honest,' said Erich. Finally he had something he could impress Hans with, but it had not worked yet.

'Huh,' Hans grunted, and carried on watching the swans. They had reached the floating house, gliding round it in a beautiful arc.

The two girls were more patient and quiet. They were actually a bit scared: they did not really like rats. Horrible creatures. Pretty much the most repulsive animals in the world. Especially those smooth, hairless tails. Ugh. And didn't they go for people? Who had said recently that they got into bedrooms and—brr—don't think about it. We should go, really—but. . . it's quite interesting, actually. And

5

the boys would laugh and rag them, too. Scaredy cats. No. . .

Fifi whispered into Luise's ear: 'I'm going to count to thirty, real slow, and if they haven't come, we'll just go. They can say what they like. OK?'

Luise just nodded, but did not look at her, fixing her large, sombre eyes on the bank, where the water stopped, the mud began, then the short, steep slope with its brown earth and free-hanging tree roots. So that was where those horrible creatures lived. Soft, warm mud. Toads. Pink worms. A little further on small fish glided through the gold-brown water. Luise scratched her bare knee in excitement, even though it did not itch. She was squatting, her arms wrapped round her legs. Her shoes were dirty yet again, and her socks, and what about the back of her skirt? She had sat down at one point. . .

'There,' said Erich, his finger shooting out towards the bottom of the bank. 'There. Look. . .'

'You were lucky,' said Fifi. 'I was about to count to thirty, real slow, and. . .'

'Shut up, you idiot. You'll scare them away.'

It was beginning to get dark. You couldn't quite make everything out. But something was moving. Grey. Small. Under the tree roots. And again. There were two. And another. Three. They were coming nearer. The children froze, and stared.

'They come every evening,' whispered Erich all of a sudden in triumph, looking at Hans, as if he had made the rats himself.

Hans nodded gravely. 'Just look at those tails,' he said. They looked at the tails. The length of a finger, grey, hairless, twitching back and forth. 'Lie on your front,' hissed Hans.

6

Without making a sound they did as they were told, poking their heads over the bank.

Then Luise suddenly screamed, shrill and piercing, as if bitten by a snake, in great distress. The rats leaped into the water and disappeared.

'You idiot!' shouted Hans. 'Now they've gone.'

'That was a stupid thing to do, screaming like that,' said Erich.

Luise was beside herself with tears. 'It looked at me, with its little eyes, real nasty, and then it started to open its mouth, like this, and there were its teeth. It was going to bite me, I'm sure of it.'

'Damn it, you can't do anything with girls. Come on, Erich, we're going to the harbour. The *Adelaide*'s still there. You haven't seen it yet. Let's leave this pair of cry-babies. Rotten pair. I've had enough of you.' Erich stuck out his lower lip in scorn and went after Hans, his hands in his trouser pockets.

Luise had almost stopped crying. 'It gave me such a nasty look with its little eyes,' she said to herself.

'Never mind,' said Fifi. 'We've got to go home anyway.'

They looked around. The sun had gone and the water lay black in the town moat, you couldn't see very deep now, and it had shone such a golden brown. Mist, rising gently from the water, lay thickly over it. The trees in the park were starting to form heavy, dark clumps, the windmill on the hill raised its brown sails, soft and reproachful, in the warm, blue, smoky sky. From the harbour road glimmered the little flames in the lanterns. They would soon flare up.

Up on the path sat an old man on a bench, calmly looking straight ahead, his hands on his stick. Fifi skipped up to him, carelessly.

'Sir, what time is it?'

'Half past seven,' said the man, pressing the little button which flicked open the lid of his gold watch. Papa's watch isn't as big as that, and not made of gold either, or silver for that matter, thought Fifi. 'Thank you,' she said quietly.

'Wait a minute,' said the old man, fixing his blank grey eyes on her. 'What were you doing by the moat? What were you looking for?'

Fifi was silent, and looked at the ground, smiling.

'You wanted to see the rats, didn't you? Out with it.'

Fifi said nothing.

'I know: you wanted to see the rats,' said the old man. 'Do you like them then?'

'No,' said Fifi without looking up.

'Thought as much,' said the old man. He chuckled suddenly. 'You always want to see disgusting things, you children. Haven't you got anything better to look at besides rats?'

'No, we have,' said Fifi and quickly ran away, without once glancing at the old man. Luise was still standing in the same place, but she looked happy again now.

'It's already half seven. Come on, quick.'

They followed the moat and came to the street. The lamps were burning now, and even the tram—a Number 1 had just gone past and stopped under the railway bridge—had its lights on.

Frau Jacobi got out. She was carrying several packages. Fifi and Luise curtseyed politely, in an affected way. 'Good evening, children. Still out and about? Come on, off to bed with you,' she threatened in a friendly voice. Mama will strike a different tone. Only other ladies had this nice way

8

of talking. But I still prefer Mama. I wouldn't like to have Frau Jacobi. Luise yawned. At the street corner they parted. They briefly shook hands.

The Number 1 tram which Frau Jacobi had been on went along the harbour road. It stopped. A drunken man came out of Bellmann's restaurant. The moment the door opened the sound of an orchestrion and laughter poured out. The conductor held the drunken man back, forcing him physically off the running board.

'I'm not having you on.'

'I. . . I. . . What do you mean. . . I've got the money. . . You bastard. . .'

'Off. Do you hear?' A bell. The tram moved on. The man was left behind, hurling abuse. 'Don't want the lot of them filling the carriage with puke,' said the conductor to Oskar and Anton. The two students nodded earnestly, in sage agreement. The conductor looked at their large suitcases.

'Going on the *Adelaide*?' he asked.

'That's right,' said Anton. 'Rotterdam.'

'I envy you, on the sea like this in September,' said the conductor. 'If only.'

'Yes, we're really looking forward to it,' said Anton, and looked somewhat guiltily through the window. They were just passing the Astoria. The woman in the box office pulled back the curtain and pushed the window up halfway.

'There's a fantastic fight today between Dieckmann and Alvaroz, the champion wrestlers. You know. . .'

Anton raised his eyes as if trying to remember. 'No, I don't think so.'

'On the *Adelaide*, eh,' said the conductor. 'Then you'll be getting acquainted with Captain Martens.' He laughed to himself. 'The man with the fancy stewards.'

'What do you mean?' asked Oskar.

'You'll see. And that fat little Nelly, too. That'll be fun. She always gets to sit on the red plush in the saloon.'

'Who's Nelly?' asked Anton.

'You'll soon see for yourselves, gentlemen. One thing's for certain: never a dull moment on the *Adelaide*.' And with grin on his face, the conductor went along the car.

'Bit disconcerting,' said Anton. 'What was all that about the ship?'

'Leave him,' said Oskar. 'He's only trying to spoil it. He's envious.'

'Shame we leave in the dark—down the river, the estuary, out to sea—we'll hardly see a thing.'

'Yes. Stupid.'

'But then. . . the dark has its attractions. I shan't sleep much tonight.'

'Let's just wait and see, shall we?' said Oskar. 'Don't go over the top.'

The old man was still sitting on the bench, his hands on his stick, his hat next to him. He cast a calm, vacant gaze around. He just sat there. That was his life now. He sat there on that bench and looked around, taking in whatever happened and watching the evening draw on. He sat in the park, behind him the windmill on the hill, before him the grassy bank and the moat, and over there the railway embankment, behind which you could just see the first floor of the houses in Olbersstrasse, their white walls now dull in the dusk. He had watched the sun disappear behind the houses, the nursemaids with prams and children playing games had long since left the park, the water in the moat had turned black and the air soft and smoky and the sky a greyish blue. Some time before a little girl had asked him the time, and then promptly ran away again, really fled. Yes, they all went off, just left him sitting there. Even Karl and Berta didn't care for him very much, they visited him less and less in the evenings. Well, it's true, he couldn't offer them much, they'd rather go to the pictures.

From over on the harbour road came the dull sound of cars rumbling by. People were leaving work. The sausage-stand which stood underneath the railway bridge was surrounded by workmen. They bought the fat, red, peppery sausages, and he could hear the echo of their laughter. A dog, without its owner, padded past him on the dusky path, its head up in the air, following a scent. It knew where it was going. Everyone was going home. But what am I supposed to do at home? Sit in a dark room and look down at the street until it's time to go to bed? And then not be able to go to sleep? I'll sit here a while longer, sit and wait, but nobody comes. It's dreadful, nobody comes. But perhaps somebody will, perhaps that young man will come and I can have a few words with him. Isn't that him over there? No, it's not him. Look at that! The swans brushing against each other, snuggling, rubbing their necks together: someone's nocturnal pleasures already under way, then. Oh, they've stopped now, split up, swimming in gentle circles round their house. Was that it? That was quick. They head for their house, climb up the little wooden plank, lie down, gaze once more across the thick, tarlike surface of the water and tuck their heads under their wings. Sleep now. They stay outside the whole night. I should really be going. I'll just wait for the eight o'clock train. I wonder if that young man will come?

It will be a little while yet. He is still anxiously pounding the streets, his hands in his coat pockets. There is a strange, restless feeling in his legs. And his eyes glisten. He always takes the same route. Every day. Along the streets, across the embankment to the river. And then he stands on the bridge, watches the water rush underneath, red in the evening glow, black at night, it surges round the piers, whispering incomprehensibly to him. And he walks into the park, shares a few words with the old man who always sits there, always on the same bench, an old man who is unspeakably bored and doesn't want to let him go. Is he the only person he can talk to all day? And the old man can hardly conceal his joy when he comes. But today Peter doesn't want to listen to his desperate, empty chatter; he doesn't want to speak to him at all. Even I only talk to him because I don't have anyone else. No, today for once I shall walk past him. Say hello and walk past.

He turned off the street, heaving with traffic, into the 'Seefahrt'. He enjoyed walking through the large courtyard of this institution, where the widows of seamen lived. It was so wonderfully quiet and dead. You instantly felt the deep peace of their deadness. In some of the rooms the old dears had already lit their lamps and were having supper; the windows were open, but there was not a sound to be heard. The occasional chink of a plate, a spoon and knife knocking together; the shrill voice of a parrot from a dark corner, vain and insolent: 'Little Lora, little Lora. . .' Some of the women had still not lit their lamps and were sitting at the window, staring out motionless, in a stupor; two hunched, round, black figures slowly walked along the wall of the building, another two stood before a little front garden, whispering and tittering, their bonnets waggling like cockscombs, and there was the sound of a little fountain which stood, foliage up to the rim, in the middle of a tiny patch of dark grass. Here it is quiet; here it is dead. They're simply no longer alive. Their children have left, their husbands lie at the bottom of the sea perhaps, but they are still in the harbour. They have the parrot they used to take with them when they still travelled with their husbands. They have little shells and pieces of coral on their dressing tables, and they doze away.

Then he was outside again, and he finally reached the park. After the park it was the harbour road, the river, then who knows where. And that's where he wanted to go: anywhere. But then he saw the old man in the distance. He was sitting on the bench as usual. Motionless, his hands on his stick, his hat on the bench beside him, he looked over at Peter, and as Peter tried walking quickly past with a 'hello' he called: 'You must have a moment to spare. Come on. I've been waiting for you for a long time.'

And when Peter had sat down: 'You should have seen. Children looking in the water over the bank. What were they looking for? Rats! Children, I ask you. Amazing what attracts them.'

'Rats? How funny!' said Peter, absent-mindedly.

He looked at the moat. There, round the bend, something black had appeared. A boat and a man rowing it with gentle strokes, splashing quietly. A broad boat, tarred and black. The rowlocks creaked. The man was wearing a large tapered straw hat.

'Who's that?'

'Don't you know the park keeper? You surprise me. Once a week he goes along the moat, making sure everything's all right. Checks the duck and the swan houses. He lives up there.' He pointed over his shoulder with his thumb.

'In the windmill? What about the miller?'

'Didn't you know the mill isn't in use any more? Been dead for ten years. It's just decoration now, a theatrical backdrop. And somewhere for the park keeper to live. Strange feller. I could tell you a few things about him. . .'

But Peter did not want to hear any more. He knew these interminable stories. 'Sorry, but I have to go. Things to do.'

'What things? I hope you don't mind my asking, or is it private, what you. . .'

'Nothing important, nothing particular.'

'Nothing particular, nothing important? Ha, I know what you mean. I was just the same. You're busy tonight. Say no more. I was young once, too. But times change.' The old man chortled. 'Good luck. All the best.'

Peter felt sick. 'You misunderstand. Honestly. I just wanted. . . I'm going to the cinema. Not what you think.'

'And why not? No need for false modesty. We're both men. Course, the cinema's not without its. . . gets you in the mood. Yes, all the best. You'll be fine. I'll keep me fingers crossed.'

Peter hurried away. Disgusting. That's the last time I sit next to him. He walked along the moat to the harbour road, and when he reached the railway bridge, just as he went past the sausage-stand, the eight o'clock train trundled over the bridge. It went along the embankment, past the houses in Olbersstrasse, their façades dully lit by the lamplight, and its headlights flew in long streaks through the water in the moat. That was the signal for the old man to get up. Slowly, hesitantly, he would make his way home. For a short time he stood where he was, looking over towards the park keeper. His boat was nearing the swan house, and the swan woke up. Took its head out from under its wing, stretched its neck towards the park keeper and, with great, silent strokes, flapped its wings. The old man watched as the swan laid its head on the park keeper's hand; the park keeper tickled it gently under its bill. . . Finally, the old man really had to go. He dreaded his room, with its stiff chairs, silent walls, the pictures of people long dead on the wall. But maybe Karl and Berta would stop by and they could have a chat, maybe they'd already be there when he arrived, maybe they'd already have gone again because he wasn't there. He suddenly quickened his step. . .

But he need not have hurried: they were not sitting in his room waiting for him, and they would not come later either. He would have to see how he got through the evening alone. Karl and Berta were not even in town. It was Karl's afternoon off, and they had gone off on the steamer, downriver. They were just coming back. Berta was not thinking about her father, or even her husband, who was sitting at the table out the back, on deck, his head heavy from the strawberry punch and the bright afternoon sun. He had closed his eyes and was gently snoring.

She felt nothing other than the presence of the man she was dancing with. It was the ship's helmsman. He had been watching her all afternoon and now he was dancing with her. Her head was tipped back, her mouth slightly open, and her close-cropped hair fluttered in the balmy evening breeze. She looked at him in an amorous, seductive way, his strong, weathered face, the bright blue eyes, the firm muscles she kept pressing against, it all appealed to her.

'I'm really quite tipsy,' she said. 'I kept eating the strawberries.'

'That's dangerous,' he laughed. 'They soak up the alcohol.'

'I know, I know. But they're so lovely. I'm such a silly thing.'

The band was playing a tango, and the couples spun in tight rows under the canopy and in among the tables. The riverbank passed by soft and flat, cows stood in the dark fields, and on the beach there were still bathers, shrieking and waving. Sailing boats slipped smoothly past.

'Come on,' said the helmsman, taking her firmly by the arm.

They went downstairs. 'Watch out. Don't trip. One step at a time. . .'

They walked along the corridor.

He opened a door. 'My cabin.'

'No, I'm not going in there.' Berta was suddenly scared. He pulled her in; she resisted, holding on to the door frame. Then she gave in. She threw herself onto the bed, laughing terribly. 'What a rotter you are. A real little swine. Taking a poor woman unawares like that.' Then she threw herself on him, kissed him, ran her hands over his arms, his face, and pulled him down onto the bed. The steamer carried on. On the bank farmhouses, dockyards, factories slipped by. The band played, and the glow of the town lay on the horizon.

To begin with they had watched a drunk for a while. He was trying to board a tram, but the conductor would not let him on. He stood in the middle of the street, swearing and hurling abuse at the tram as it disappeared. Hans positioned himself quite close, so as to hear everything he said. They even followed him as he staggered along the street, expressing his indignation to passers-by. No one would listen to him, but Hans nodded wholeheartedly at his blathering. The drunk was still cursing the tram conductor, and little Hans gazed up, engrossed, at his distraught, red face, his vacant eyes. He pinched Erich's side in delight. Then Hans wanted to look at the smart car which stood in front of the harbour customs house, gleaming dark blue in the glow of the arc lamp. A distinguished gentleman in a yellow coat had disappeared into the customs house, and the chauffeur, in green livery and sparkling polished gaiters, was walking up and down in front of the red-brick wall. Hans looked in the car, then at the little silver eagle on the bonnet, lifted a flap and squeezed the horn, which honked gently. 'That'll do,' said the chauffeur arrogantly.

And on they went, where they saw the door of a public house open—smoke, men round little tables, bar, beer glasses, electric piano, hubbub—they looked at the window displays of the cigar shops, the enormous cigars, dark as chocolate, the leaf tobacco, pipes, colourful plaster Indians, the miniature tropical landscapes on the inside lids of the open cigar boxes.

While Hans dreamily lost himself in the radiant colours of a tobacco harvest, Erich turned round suddenly to see a policeman in the middle of the street, directing traffic with sharp movements of his arm, and the distinguished yellow gentleman coming out of the customs house with a customs official, who looked through his spectacles with stern disapproval and gravely bade goodbye to the distinguished gentleman. Cars trundled past, trams. Sailors and dock workers went by; it was almost dark now, the sky deep blue and oppressive, the white light of the arc lamp flowed down onto the policeman, across the street, over the dull red wall of the customs house and trickled away into grass, bushes and trees, over where the railway embankment rose up. It was late, it was night, and in the distance there was the sound of a steamer. Above them hung a clock: quarter past eight.

Erich quickly pulled Hans over. 'Come on, it's late. We need to go home.' He pointed at the large, dully lit clock face above them.

'Home? Now? No way. What about the *Adelaide*?'

'We can see it tomorrow.'

'No, it's leaving tonight. And anyway, we're on our way there now.'

Hans looked at him with a mixture of disdain and encouragement. Erich could not resist. He could never resist that cheeky, arrogant face of Hans's. They quickened their pace. But in front of the Astoria, the façade of which was now brightly lit, they had to stop. The entire wall was covered with a gigantic poster. Wrestling! Dieckmann versus Alvaroz! They stood opposite each other, their bodies bent and heads threatening like bulls. Their flesh florid pink, with enormous muscles, their trunks bright red and blue. Hans stared at the two figures for a long time. It had nothing to do with enjoyment: he felt a deep respect. Erich was hugely impressed. Here they were, and now they were going to go further and further away, away from home. Strangers crowded round the Astoria box office. Out there lay the harbour with ships that sailed the ocean, the world. He felt so alone. And meanwhile his mother would be having tea with his father; his fried egg and potatoes would be cold, and his mother would cover them with a plate. He could still make it. But he had to wander about here, there was nothing else for it. Did he want to lose Hans, this one, great friendship with someone he envied in everything? Impossible. He gently put his arm round his friend's slim, bare neck.

'Get off. Stop being such a girl.' Contempt swept across Hans's pale face, his grey eyes flashed and a small, sharp crease appeared, just above the bridge of his nose, across his smooth, high forehead.

'Come on, but behave yourself.' Hans turned off suddenly into a dark, narrow side street. 'Wait for us.' He went a short distance and stood in a corner by the wall. The delicate streak shimmered pure and bright in the lamplight. Erich saw a man coming. He whistled a warning. Hans laughed mockingly. The man stopped, waiting to tell Hans off. But then he walked up to that snooty man. He came right up to him, bold as brass, crowing. Then walked off. Just left him standing there.

'As if I couldn't pee there,' he said to Erich, shaking his head. 'What was that about? Huh?'

Erich said nothing. What Hans did was fine, right, and brave.

They arrived at the entrance to the harbour. In the distance funnels and masts rose up out of the depths of the harbour over the quay.

'There's the *Adelaide*. Lights on already, too.'

Frau Jacobi climbed the dark stairs. She knew every step. Her packages bumped, rustling, against the handrail. I'll go in again, she thought. She liked showing her sympathy regularly. I'm a very attentive person. She rang the Mahlers' doorbell. The door opened and there stood Frau Mahler in the black of the narrow corridor. Only the dull glimmer of her pale face could be seen.

'Well, dear? How are things?'

Frau Mahler was silent a moment, then sobbed quietly.

'Come in. . .'

'No, no. I just wanted to know. I've got to give Herr Berg his tea.' She shook her packages. 'These are his.'

'We're near the end. He's just fading away.'

'Good Lord! Are you sure?'

'I just can't believe it. He's actually dying. The doctor looked so queer. He's quite peaceful but doesn't say anything any more. What should I do? I just don't know.'

'You poor thing. Be brave. Hope for the best. One never knows. And I'm always here to help, you know. I'll come back down once Herr Berg's had his tea.'

'How that man can still play his flute,' said Frau Mahler, bitterly.

'What? Is he? Oh! I shall go straight up and. . .'

Frau Jacobi jabbered away, but Frau Mahler just nodded absently, not listening, and went back in. She was drawn to the deathbed.

'I'll be back.' Frau Jacobi went up to her flat. Herr Mahler's bedroom was directly below hers. That meant that tonight she might be sleeping over a corpse. Not a pleasant thought. There wouldn't be much of a funeral. He'd been retired ten years. They wouldn't make much of a fuss when the old boy disappeared from the scene. A cheap little announcement in the paper, a couple of wreaths, and the vicar certainly wasn't about to make himself hoarse with the eulogy. Do I have a black dress? I'll wear my blue suit. Yes, and the brown hat. I can take the feather off and put a black ribbon round it, yes and I still have my black gloves. I don't need to be all in black. It's not as if he's a relative. Right. Berg. I shall have to tell him. Gently, but firmly. A nice lodger, it's true. But this is too much. He's a considerate man and will understand. . . He doesn't know yet just how bad things are with the old boy.

She opened the front door and immediately heard the long, clear notes. She quickly put the packages down, took off her coat and knocked. Berg did not let her coming in disturb him. 'Just a moment,' he said, without looking at her. He was standing by the open window, below him the gardens, beyond the back wall of the houses, sending clear, gentle notes out into the night. In front of him was a music stand with a sheet of paper, but he surely couldn't see any more here in the dark; he must be playing from memory. 'He's just so different from me,' Frau Jacobi felt suddenly, as she looked at his grave, motionless face. A strand of black hair lay across his domed, white forehead. His neck, worryingly long and thin, protruded from an open shirt collar. The music had come to an end; Berg lowered the black, silver-keyed flute and turned to Frau Jacobi with a strange, pitiless look. His sunken cheeks and the dull smile which spread over his broad, thin mouth gave Frau Jacobi little confidence.

'Well?'

'I'll get tea now.'

'Good.'

'And, er, the gentleman downstairs. . . You know how ill he is. . . He'll probably die soon. . .'

Calm and grave, Herr Berg looked out of the window, across the gardens. A warm, gentle breeze ruffled the leaves of the trees, still green and full in September.

'Pity.' He shrugged his narrow, bony shoulders.

'I just wanted to tell you,' whispered Frau Jacobi, intimidated. She could not cope with the man. She disappeared.

And as she stood in the kitchen, he started playing again. Long, clear notes, calm, grave and solemn.

Frau Jacobi went in again and this time did not wait for Berg to stop; she interrupted the music, with muted indignation.

'Herr Berg, please. He's right under us, and may die any moment. . .'

Berg carried on playing. 'Yes, and?'

'Do you not feel it inappropriate?'

'I'm playing Bach,' he said calmly, unmoved. His long, thin, emaciated fingers rose and fell slowly over the keys of the flute. He was looking across the gardens, over the houses, off into the open, into the night.

'Bach, yes, very nice. But at this particular moment in time. . . Have you no feelings? I always thought you were such a refined man, a man'—Frau Jacobi herself did not know why she suddenly said this—'far superior to me. Well?'

Berg lowered the flute and smiled at her again, strangely. Frau Jacobi was startled at the beauty of his long, pale, sharply contoured face, she could not stand that pure, grey, penetrating gaze and looked away.

'One can always play Bach, should always play Bach,' he said with absolute certainty. 'In life and in death.'

'I don't understand,' said Frau Jacobi, completely helpless. 'I'm too stupid for all that.'

'But it's really very simple,' said Herr Berg.

It was all too strange and disturbing for Frau Jacobi. 'As far as I'm concerned, you can carry on playing. I shan't say any more about it. I'm just a stupid woman who meant well,' she said, shaking her head, and, overwhelmed, she went. While she made tea for Herr Berg, the incomprehensible notes of the flute reached her, bright, admonishing. I shall see to it that I get another lodger, she thought.

Herr Berg carried on playing; he played the whole evening. He always did and today was no exception. Clear, constant, the gentle intervals of the cool, silvery notes floated over the gardens, mixing, melting into the evening air. But who heard these notes, really heard them, who could understand their terrible message, their clear lament? The dying man did not hear them, could not hear them: he had already fallen into all too deep a sleep, otherwise he would perhaps have been the person best able to grasp these notes. Other people hardly heard them. But little Luise, leaning at the open window in her nightdress, understood the music; she thought it very beautiful, and understood it perfectly. She rested her head in her hand and dreamed down into the garden. The notes took a gentle, steady path, the soft evening breeze rustling the trees in the garden and bearing off the scent of grass, flowers and leaves. The gardens lay there dark green and obscure, trees, bushes, black fences, soft-edged lawns, children's climbing frames. Lights burned in some of the windows of the houses opposite, and people went silently back and forth. In the distance the sound of music on the radio seemed to accompany the flute. Luise breathed in the rich, sour smell from the stables of the carriage company next door. The carts stood silently in the yard, their shafts hanging down, the horses in their stalls giving the occasional snort and striking the ground with their hooves. The stable boy crossed the yard with a lamp, shining it here and there, went into the stables where, for brief moments, you could see a pale heap of hay, panelled walls with harnesses, a horse's broad, gleaming rump. Everything then sank again into soft, rippling, flowing night, and Luise floated off again with the music, on silver paths. Suddenly she started. She saw the rats again. The evil little gimlet eyes, sharp as needles, and a horrible grey lip curled up to reveal cruel teeth, gently hissing. Luise was suddenly scared of the night, of being alone. She longed for her mother, a locked room, a feeling of comfort, when she quickly looked into the neighbouring garden. And there was something to console and calm her, a peaceful scene.

There, at the bottom of the garden, under the leafy pergola, sat Herr Hennicke, her geography teacher, with his two sons. A paraffin lamp stood in the middle of the table, spreading a warm, yellow light. The lamp flickered, and Herr Hennicke carefully turned it down. In front of him a book lay open, from which he was reading. His sons, two gangly seventeen-year-olds with fair hair and glistening, pimply faces, had their heads propped up in their hands, and listened contentedly to his words. They looked out into the dark garden, or further still. Herr Hennicke wore spectacles, and his smooth, rosy skin, like that of a child, glowed. There was a silver shimmer to his grey hair. Herr Hennicke loved far-off lands, travel, adventure, the sea, ships, but he had never left his home town. He had become a geography teacher out of longing. As he was unable to travel, he read books and travelled in his mind. He preferred this method. Everything went much more smoothly that way. In the evening he would read to his sons, but during the day he often stood in the harbour, watching the ships. He knew every ship which went in and out. He was allowed to enter the harbour at any time, even reaching places where mere mortals could not, due to his being friends with the customs inspector. The latter felt sorry for him and allowed him access. So Herr Hennicke would often sit on a wooden pallet or a bale of cotton, his hand under his chin, smoking, and stare at the bustling harbour. Everyone at the harbour knew him.

Herr Hennicke interrupted his reading, his mind wandering for a moment. 'The *Adelaide* leaves today, at half past eleven,' he said quietly. His sons nodded as, for a short while, Herr Hennicke watched the *Adelaide* depart. The notes from Herr Berg's flute, tender and light, swept around him, transforming into the silver wake of the ship.

Then he read on: 'When we came to the beach a second time, the coast looked completely different. One is not aware of such a landscape, we noted, in a storm—grey, rainy days, thick clouds, fog, all those features of the North—only in glorious weather. The smooth sea lay bright blue and translucent. Gentle waves rippled on the beach, and one could see, in the crystal-clear waters, little pink shells, crabs, and the wonderfully light veil-like forms of floating jellyfish. My enchanting friend, Maio, by now completely trustworthy, laughed at me with his white teeth, threw his spear and, with unbelievable accuracy, hit one of the gigantic fish which flashed by. His gleaming brown body was almost Grecian in its beauty. He led me to understand, by means of expressive hand gestures, that. . .' Footsteps crunched on the gravel and Herr Hennicke looked up. The customs inspector was coming, stiff and grave. Herr Hennicke quickly shut the book, blushing like a boy caught playing with a doll. 'That's enough for today,' he said, with a certain imposed bluster. 'Leave us alone now, boys.' His sons lolled about in their seats for a time, yawning without covering their mouths, before standing up and disappearing with gangly movements, weary and dream-fuddled.

The customs inspector looked at the book scornfully and burst out laughing: 'Head still full of that nonsense? Some teacher you are. Instead of opening their eyes in a timely manner and steeling them for the struggles of life, you. . . Oh, never mind. There's no point.' Wearily, he shook his head, and cast a sullen look at his friend through his spectacles. Herr Hennicke was still blushing slightly, and his eyes stared at the burning wick. The flame rose up again and he turned it down, pleased to have something to do. Herr Berg's music swept by, clear and sorrowful.

The customs inspector considered Herr Hennicke a clueless child. He, on the other hand, was a man of the world. He had worked in customs for twenty-five years, and knew a thing or two about it! He had an extraordinary ability in detecting smugglers. Oh, he knew what he was doing all right. Nothing escaped his eyes. Maybe they had become too sharp: they saw some things a little too well, and other things not at all. How could he help but pour scorn on Herr Hennicke and his children's books and old wives' tales? But he still loved him. He was so sorry for him. Good

God, if he could only open his eyes one of these days. It didn't bear contemplating.

Herr Hennicke was listening to the flute, his head raised. He swayed in time to the music.

The customs inspector listened as well; it was very beautiful, he loved music. Yet he still said: 'The man is obsessed with the flute. Playing has gone to his head. Would you mind?'

'What?' asked Herr Hennicke, distracted.

The customs inspector had undone the top button of his green uniform. 'It digs in when you're sitting down. As you know.'

'We *are* old friends,' said Herr Hennicke.

The customs inspector snorted bitterly. 'They swan up in their great, fancy cars, with their chauffeurs, an elegant yellow macinktosh, but you've only to look a little closer and . . .'

Herr Hennicke laid his hand on the customs inspector's arm: 'Leave it now. Don't think about it.'

'Yes, let's leave it. Filth and more filth,' murmured the customs inspector. He wanted to carry on complaining, couldn't really. The two friends smiled at each other. The clear sound of Herr Berg's flute reached them, and the customs inspector stretched, sprawling out on the bench, his uniform gaped open to reveal his snow-white shirt, his golden epaulettes flashed. 'One can be human here, at least.'

They sat restfully in silence in the light of the lamp under the pergola, enjoying the peace and the music.

Then the flute suddenly broke off, in the middle of a rising sequence of notes.

'Now he's stopped, and right in the middle, stupid fellow,' said the customs inspector in a plaintive voice. 'And it was so lovely, too.'

Frau Jacobi had switched on the light. Herr Berg did not want to play any more. He sat on the sofa and, with a smile, watched Frau Jacobi set the table for tea. Usually, at this point she was in the habit of saying: 'Now, eat up. I've laid out all these lovely things for you, then I have to take most of them away again. You eat less and less. Little more than a bird.' But today she said nothing. Only when she had finished did she look at him reproachfully for a moment. His white shirt collar was thrown wide open, and she could see his pale, bony chest. She could see dark little furrows on it. 'Well, eat nicely, now,' she said quickly and left. She suddenly realised: he won't last much longer either. Another one with a death sentence. And there he is, calmly playing the flute. Back in her room, she could still see his faint smile.

'Mama, will you look at this child,' said Luise's sister. 'At the window in her nightdress. If she doesn't catch cold, then I don't know what.' Luise had begun to nod off. Her arms lay on the windowsill and her head lay on her arms.

'What are you doing, child?' Her mother took her under the arms and gently lifted her into bed.

'I fell asleep,' said Luise, yawning. 'First I heard Herr Hennicke's talking and then I fell asleep.' Luise was more awake again now and snuggled down in bed.

'A quick prayer, and then back to sleep.' Her mother and sister both stood at the foot of the bed; her mother had already put her hands together in the customary way. Anni, however, simply rested her hands on the bedstead. Luise noticed.

'Anni isn't putting her hands together,' said Luise triumphantly.

This annoyed Anni. 'What's that got to do with you? It doesn't matter whether I put my hands together or not.' Embarrassed, she put her hands one on top of the other.

'That's not putting them together properly,' Luise persisted.

'That's enough. "I'm tired." Now, come on. Stop fussing.' Her mother had already closed her eyes. She always did that when she prayed.

Luise began the usual words, dreary and detached, in a half-voice. Anni needn't think she was such a silly goose that she couldn't see through the whole charade. She'd spoken to Hans about praying only today and they'd agreed that she was much too old for it.

She suddenly stopped, giggling into the bedclothes.

'Er, what's all this laughing during your prayers?' Her mother had become quite upset.

'Oh, Mama. Anni looks so funny.'

Anni had tried to keep her eyes fixed on the window. Now she had to laugh, too. She was annoyed, but couldn't help it.

'Mama, the cheek of it. Well, you can do it on your own. I'd rather be next door anyway.' She understood Luise only too well. Mama didn't feel it: you can't pray with children at this age. She'd done it with her, too. Until she kept on laughing. . .

Their mother had had enough trying to pray with Luise today. 'Any solemnity has now gone,' she said. 'I shouldn't really give you a kiss today,' she said, bending over the bed.

Luise hugged her tight, pressing her cheeks against her mother's head.

'Mama,' she whispered. 'I will pray, but quietly. Mama, please, can I pray quietly from now on? Just to myself? I will do it.'

As her mother sat down at the table with Anni, she said: 'I worry about that child.'

'Oh, she's just getting older, that's all.'

Luise was happy and relieved. She was pleased she had told Mama the truth. She stretched out her legs and pulled the covers up to her neck. She could hear the murmur of voices outside. There was talking from under Herr Hennicke's pergola. The horses at the carriage company gave the occasional snort, and then came the sound of the lovely music again. Herr Berg had finished tea, Frau Jacobi had cleared away, it was dark in the room again and Herr Berg was standing in his spot by the window and playing his flute. In the next room her mother and Anni were talking. The door always had to be ajar, so Luise could hear voices and see a bit of light.

'He didn't want to go, but he had to,' said Anni. 'They're important to Georg, these dos.'

'Sounds very reasonable,' said her mother. 'He has to, as a teacher.'

'You know what I'm really scared of? Him coming home drunk, or even just a bit tipsy. I hate that. "Anni," he said, when he was going out, "I might have to have a drink when I go bowling. I can't not drink, if the others are. I hardly touch alcohol any other time. I'm sure it'll be fine. But don't be annoyed if I do." I was disgusted. I told him: I don't believe this. On no account are you. . .'

Her mother smiled charitably. 'Oh Anni, you'll get used to it.'

Luise had meanwhile fallen asleep. Herr Hennicke and the customs inspector were still sitting outside. Herr Berg played Bach, and Anni realised it was time to go home. She put her cap on over her short, black glossy hair and gave her mother a fleeting kiss. Her dark eyes looked bleak. 'I really am quite scared.' Her mother patted her encouragingly on the shoulder: 'Now, now.'

'Oh Mama, everything had been so perfect up till now.'

'Good God, you've only been married a couple of months. . .'

Anni left. She walked slowly home through the streets. She planned to go to bed straight away. After all, what was the point of sitting in the flat all alone?

And Herr Berg played, played out across the gardens. The dying man did not hear him, could not hear him, and Luise did not hear him any more either. But the customs inspector and Herr Hennicke, still chatting in low voices, heard him, at ease under the pergola, the notes floating around them like spirits. The notes, measured and austere, even reached the ear of the old man sitting alone in his room. But only his ear, not his heart. The old man was slowly walking up and down. When he got to the far end of the room, which looked out over the garden, he could hear the flute more clearly. He looked across the gardens, towards the far wall. He heard the notes, the trees rustling gently, but it meant nothing to him and he walked to the front of the house again, looked down into the street. People were walking by, in the distance he could hear car horns, tram noises, the rumble of traffic. In other houses, families sat round tables in lit rooms. Courting couples went whispering by, everyone spoke in hushed tones and had something to say. The old man sat down in the large wingback chair by the window. His rooms were dark and only a thin strip of light fell through the curtain onto the wall. He sketched the pattern of the curtain with his finger. Like a thin veil, the pattern was cast across the picture of his late wife. With an austere look of indifference, her black eyes stared out through the veil, past him, into the distance. He stood up again. Went back and forth. Switched on the light and fetched a game of patience from the sideboard. He laid out the cards for a short while, but soon lost interest in the game and tried reading the newspaper. Then he switched the light off again and began wandering about once more. Karl and Berta hadn't come, and they wouldn't come now either. Should he go to bed? No, better not. All that lying there with your eyes open, tossing and turning, was dreadful. It'd be better if he just wandered about the rooms. If only that man would stop that interminable flute-playing. He couldn't bear it any more. He always played the same thing. The clock in the glass cabinet, a golden blacksmith with a hammer, struck the hour with a bright, trembling blow. Good God, still so early! How slowly time creeps by!

Yes, time passed, too slow for one man, for another too quick. And yet it passed neither quickly nor slowly, but at a constant, continuous, remorseless pace, as strict and regular as the notes of Herr Berg's flute which floated out over the gardens, rising, falling, unending, in rigid uniformity. And this passing, this flow of time was neither happy nor sad, it just simply was: unfathomable. Time moves in everything, moves everyone and everything, and everyone moves in it; it moved in the water and the trees and the wind, in pulsing blood and beating hearts, it moved and it surged and raced, it raced out of the dark and back into the dark, without beginning or end. The day had run its course, night had come, just a night, one of countless nights, but the like of which would never be repeated. Its effect on life would never be the same again, and whoever was not alive to it, whether dreaming or waking, whoever missed it had missed it for ever, and his life was slightly, imperceptibly slightly, the poorer. A day had past and a night had come—important, unimportant—a rich, warm September night: it was now complete. It surged past, broad and heavy. It filled the streets and gardens, nestled in the trees and bushes and ruffled the leaves with its warm breath and drew the penetrating scent of flowers and grass along the streets. It sank into parks, ponds, and ditches, brooded over the harbour, the river, and squeezed under the arches of the bridge. The muted water ran past the piers. And the town tried to repress it: with lanterns and arc lamps, with music and conversation—but the night was stronger. It filled everything, enveloped everything, plunging it into deeper and deeper blackness. It was the soft, rich, elemental stream on which everything rested, into which everything sank; it loosened people's limbs, made them feel sleepy and full. Many were already asleep, Luise was already asleep, the dying man was asleep, and his wife sat in the dark bedroom next to him, listening to his breathing as it grew weaker and weaker. And the seamen's widows in the 'Seefahrt', one after the other, now put out their lights and went to bed. They had not been entirely awake during the day, and now they sank into an even deeper sleep, from dream into dream. And in their dark rooms, on their dress-ing tables, lay the pieces of coral and large seashells, me-mentos of their husbands who had long lain at the bottom of the sea. Others were just coming to life, now, at night. Women walked the harbour road, casting around. They made eyes at people and called out. They stood under the lantern and next to the colourful poster-column. The great arc lamp shone purple and white. The beer halls filled up, the paper lanterns swaying when the doors opened, and the thin, shrill plink-plonk of an electric piano floated out. Smiling couples sat on the plush of the hard sofas, their hands laid on each other. Men and women crowded round the Astoria box office. They went through the archway and into the beer garden. There they sat at tables, glasses before them, cigars in their mouths, waiting for the start. Waiters dashed about and lean, red-liveried bellboys, with caps set at an angle and pale children's faces, offered chocolate and tobacco. There was a veranda along each side of the garden and people were sitting there, too. In the centre, between the tables, a raised dance floor had been erected. A jazz band sat to one side under a canopy covered with greenery. They played a rousing march as the wrestlers came out of the shadows in a long procession, their strong limbs gleam-ing in the lamplight. They walked between the tables and climbed onto the stage. They formed a line on the stage, and the announcer read out the names of those who were to fight today. Each wrestler whose name was called stepped forward, bowed with arm outstretched and the band played a fanfare. The audience applauded one, hissed or sat indif-ferently for another. Many of them looked expectantly at the programme: wrestling bouts, interspersed with variety acts and dancing up on the stage. And when things are over here, the entertainment carries on upstairs, in the theatre itself: after-hours cabaret, drinking and dancing. There's contentment for you, comfortably ensconced in your chair, with a decent swig of beer, smoking a cigar and taking things as they come. Many sailors and dock workers had come, with here and there a Chinaman, a negro. They had left their ships, which lay hulking and black down in the harbour. Only the *Adelaide* was brightly lit, the crew at work stowing the cargo. The captain appeared occasionally on the bridge and watched the large crane, creaking and clanking, lower the fat bales into the ship's hold. Erich and Hans sat on a coil of rope, surveying the scene. They looked into a cabin with its lights on. There, two men were just unpacking their cases and settling in. It was Oskar and Anton, the two students who were travelling to Rotterdam. Erich and Hans watched their silent movements with envy.

A white pleasure steamer slipped into the harbour with a gentle swoosh, its lights shimmering in the water. It drew up to the quay, and the gangplank was pushed across. People got off. Berta stood next to Karl, pale and silent. Her eyes had a peculiar sparkle. The helmsman stood on the bridge, taking the tickets. Berta let Karl go first. The helmsman whispered to her: 'Go to the Astoria. The wrestling's on, and there'll be dancing. I'll be there soon.' Berta did not look at him and carried on walking. But she had given a little nod.

The people who had been on the pleasure steamer made their way through the harbour, past the *Adelaide*, along the harbour road, past the Astoria, to restaurants and cinemas. Some went into the Astoria, while others slowly made their way home. Some, who had further to go, boarded the tram straight away, a Number 1, which was already waiting for them. They rode along the harbour. The side where the restaurants were was bright and lively, while on the other side stood the great customs house, wine-red and silent. The windows were dark. The customs inspector was sitting with Herr Hennicke under the pergola, happily chatting to his friend and every so often listening to Herr Berg, who had started playing his flute again. The tram carried on under the railway bridge. The sausage-stand under the bridge was still surrounded by people. Steam rose from the pan, and men were greedily stuffing the spicy red meat into their mouths. Next the tram went along by the park. Couples sat on the benches by the moat, their arms wrapped round each other, gazing in silence at the smooth, tar-black surface of the water. The swans' feathers shone white and voluptuous into the night. Others sat behind bushes, under trees, touching each other and giggling. Up on the hill between the two old chestnut trees the windmill rose up into the sky. A light burned on the ground floor. The park keeper had been home for some time, his rounds over, his rotten boat lying silently on the bank. He had pulled it up out of the water slightly and chained it to the grassy bank with a spike. The park keeper's pointy straw hat hung on the stand in his room, and the old man was sitting by the lamp, reading the newspaper. On the wall hung stuffed birds, brilliantly coloured ducks, a swan. His favourites which had died. The birds, dead or alive, were the only things left for him. His wife was dead, and he had thrown his daughter out of the house. She now had a little room in the harbour road, and walked the street in the evening. She was there even today, standing next to the colourful poster-column, and when she saw Peter run past her for the tenth time she called out:

'Hey, what's up with you?' She went over to him, hooked her arm through his, walking along beside him.

Peter tried to break free. 'No, no, please. . .'

'Don't be like that.'

'But I've never done it,' he said quietly.

'Then it's high time. How old are you?'

'Twenty-eight.'

'Well I never. Still a little boy, pure as the driven snow?'

Peter nodded. He felt very uneasy. Now he had what he had wanted for so long, and what he had been afraid of. A woman was hanging on his arm, and things would take their course. Finally, he was going to learn all about this. . . thing. He'd see what all the fuss was about. If I don't mess it up. She's making fun of me. She thinks I'm ridiculous, and she's right.

She had to stop for a moment and collapsed with laughter: 'I've hooked myself a right one here. A blank slate. A clueless little boy.'

Peter suddenly tore himself free and shot her a tortured, helpless look. 'I don't want to. Not today. I'll come back. I can't like this.'

She looked into his sweet, round face. His dark eyes were angry and sad, and his mouth twitched. Someone with feeling still, not cold and jaded. He really feels it. She was moved, but still found it slightly funny.

'You don't like me, then.' She stood before him suddenly like a little girl. Isolated. Vulnerable. Abandoned to brutality. Her eyes, still defiant, looked down in disappointment, her slightly upturned button nose was at odds with her sadness, and her thin, red-silk blouse flapped gently in the night breeze against her thin frame. She stared at her foot, brushing against the cobblestones. A poor, pitiable little thing, he thought. His courage came back to him.

'All right, I'll come,' he grumbled.

She rushed up to him, embraced him, whether he wanted to or not. 'You're so lovely.' They stood in the middle of the harbour road. The arc lamp shone purple and white over them. People walked past, staring in astonishment.

'If you carry on like that, I'm leaving you right here,' he said, embarrassed.

They walked on, arm in arm, along the harbour road, through the night, through the light and people. They walked under the railway bridge, past the sausage-stand. They said nothing. Then they walked through the park. She snuggled up to him and felt hidden momentarily. Peter walked with a somewhat stiff, cumbersome gait, he felt he had been presented with a problem and was anxious to know if he could solve it correctly. His broad chest rose and fell with slow, heavy breathing and his eyes stared fixedly into the darkness.

They stopped for a moment by the moat. The feathers of the swan shimmered like snow across the blackness of the water.

'Look, Papa's swan,' she whispered.

'What do you mean?'

'My father's the park keeper. The swans and ducks are his be-all and end-all.'

'Your father's the park keeper? The man in the pointy hat?'

'You know him then, my silly, old Papa?'

'I saw him this evening. He was rowing round the moat. Do you live up there, then, too? In the mill?'

'Used to, yes.' She quickly grabbed his arm. 'Come on, let's go and see what the old boy's up to. I like to look in on him in the evenings. He's so lonely now. Why he needs to behave so foolishly. . .' She pulled him up the hill. They could hardly see the way in the dark, but she knew it exactly. The sound of whispering couples, flirting, came from the benches. They could not see them properly: they merged with the bushes and trees into an indistinct blackness.

Peter only had to stand up on tiptoes to see into the parlour, but Fanny had to fetch an old crate to stand on. The park keeper was still reading the newspaper. Despite wearing spectacles, he had to lean right in over the text. His white hair was bristly and made him look stubborn. Peter saw the stuffed birds on the walls, the brilliantly coloured ducks and a great swan with its wings outstretched, high over the sofa. Its feathers were rather grey from smoke.

'He doesn't clean the animals properly any more. The swan looks filthy,' said Fanny, shaking her head. 'Even dead animals need looking after.'

'That's Mother,' she then said, pointing at a large photograph which hung over the sofa, directly behind the old man. A large, robust woman.

'Dead?' asked Peter.

'Yes, two years ago. Everything was her fault. But now she's dead, and he's got shot of me, too.'

'Wouldn't you rather go back? Perhaps he'd be pleased. . .'

'As if. He's written me letter after letter. But I don't want to.'

'But he's getting on. If you don't soon, then. . . I don't know. . .'

'If he's dead, then he's dead. Life goes on. Sometimes I do feel like going back. But then I think: no chance. My life's already a mess.'

'Go back then! Look. . .'

'What do you know about it? Don't you judge me. It's my business. Nothing to do with you. Come on, let's go to my room.'

She held his arm tight, pulling him away, and they once again walked along in silence, through the park, past the moat, under the railway bridge and into the harbour road.

'Why don't you say anything?' She looked at him uneasily all of a sudden. 'You can't like me any more now. I know: I was horrible. Come upstairs. Still want to?'

Anxiously, Peter followed her up the steep, narrow stairs. A small red lamp cast a dim light onto the stained, pale-green walls. Downstairs was a public-house, with men laughing.

The park keeper leaned in even closer over the newspaper, holding it right up under the lamp. Aha. Here we are. He read:

RATS ERODE NEW YORK

The people of New York should have been none the wiser, but it is an issue which can no longer be ignored: John Hart, the city's Parks Commissioner, has created a specialist rat-removal committee. At a meeting of these extermination experts, at which each shared his experiences, it was confirmed that rats are not only causing trouble in Central Park and the Zoo, but that these disgusting, dangerous animals are digging a network of tunnels under the entire city, much to the horror of residents, who live in fear for their safety.

It can be concealed no longer: New York is infested with rats. Not only in parks and green spaces, in swampy areas, no: the aggressive little animals are regularly breaking into houses, sheds and apartments, in destructive, hostile packs. At issue is a particularly strong, fearless type of rat. Large, light-haired animals of this kind were reported around a year ago on Riker's Island, where they almost brought an entire village to collapse.

The brave rodent-battlers—the heroes of the moment in this city of heroes—have already begun their campaign. Initial skirmishes are over, and cost one official two fingers. The man tried to strike dead two rats on a park path, but the animals, driven into a corner, fought back. Hardly had the park keeper landed the first blow when a good dozen rats fell on him, in an attempt to climb up and bite hold of him. Only by fleeing under an artificial waterfall could the official save himself from further attack by the blood-thirsty animals and their repugnant squeaks and piercing screams.

Who can possibly gauge how many rats are involved? Some say five hundred thousand, others two million. Either way, the danger is great. New York, with dogged determination, is waging a secret rat war. Will it succeed in exorcising these creatures of the night back underground? An agonising question.

Yes, New York has had its problems. The peaceful, orderly life rightly longed for by its citizens was once jeopardised by gangsters. Then came the prohibition era and economic crises. And now, finally, the great city is being eaten away by rats. . .

The park keeper's clenched fist fell onto the table, making the lamp wobble slightly, and he cast a perplexed, disconcerted look past the walls with the stuffed birds. So. . . That was what it could come to! I knew it. They were still quite harmless at the moment, running round the edge of the moat in little packs, but they breed quickly, they'd grow, they'd get into the town, into houses. He was right to warn the authorities. One day he'd wipe that supercilious smile off their faces. They bit two fingers off that chap, the little bloodsuckers. He looked at his own hand. Between his thumb and forefinger, right through the freckles and grey hairs, were two little red lines, dried blood, and his hand was still swollen. Insolent little beasts. Shameless. Wanting to kill his lovelies. He'd put a stop to their fun. He had quietly rowed up to the duck house, carefully checked their warm, cosy boxes. There was Lilli, the brightly coloured one with the shimmering green neck, all sad and plump in the corner, staring at an egg with her shiny black eyes, an egg which the little monster was sucking out. . . And as he shot in his arm, to chase it away, it leaped onto his hand, screaming, hissing, bit hard, wriggling as it sucked, hung there as he pulled his hand out. He took the oar and hit it on the head, and the rat plopped into the water. Ha.

He stood up, tottered over to the sideboard with his broad, stooping back and took out some writing paper. He fetched the inkwell and pen-holder and wrote slowly and awkwardly in large, scrawly letters with sweeping loops:

To the City Authorities...
Esteemed Gentlemen,

I write to you again, with an urgent and most humble request for your attention. I have just read the following in the newspaper. I enclose the relevant cutting for your reference. I appeal to you that the issue is not taken lightly. . .

The beds were positioned one above the other, and Anton sat on the lower bunk. Opposite stood a small table, and behind it a sofa, on which Oskar sat. They sat in silence, their hands folded, having a little rest. On the table stood a small lamp, which cast its light on a pile of books and notebooks. Oskar intended to do some work on the journey.

'It's a too bad you have to work,' said Anton. 'I shall probably spend the whole time on deck.'

'Time management, dear chap, that's all it is. Obviously, I shall get a couple of hours of fresh air a day, but I've got work to do, too. Right. Time to wash hands and go to the dining room. Press the button.'

'Why me?' said Anton, but he stood up and pressed the bell next to the door. Underneath it read: 'Steward'.

After a while someone knocked at the door.

'Come in,' called Oskar.

The steward came in quickly and quietly, bowing low before the two of them. 'Good evening, gentlemen. I am the steward. At your service. What can I do for you?' The steward was of a delicate build, with blond, curly hair and a rosy, pockmarked face; his blue eyes looked gracious and a little apprehensive, and his pert nose curved upward somewhat impudently. He wore a white linen jacket and black trousers.

Anton stared at his soft, pockmarked face in astonishment, while Oskar said: 'Some water, please.'

'Straight away.' The steward disappeared.

'Do you know what?'

'What?' Oskar had already returned to leafing through a book.

'That was Bauer.'

'Bauer? What do you mean?'

'The steward is Bauer. Fritz Bauer. From Marburg. Don't you remember? A couple of years ago, he was always in the History Department. He looks devilishly similar.'

'Nonsense.'

'I'm going to ask him.'

'Oh, don't go getting mixed up with these people.'

A knock, and the steward came back in with two water jugs. Anton watched his supple movements. Anton stood up and stepped closer to him. His round, honest face smiled in a friendly manner, slightly ashamed. He hesitated before saying: 'Listen, you remind me of someone. But it can't be. Are you Fritz Bauer, who used to study in Marburg? Funny if you are.'

The steward turned red and smiled, alarmed and confused. 'Yes. It's me. But how could you. . . I don't remember at all, I mean, God, you can't remember everyone. . .'

'It's really you? How extraordinary. I noticed straight away. Didn't I immediately say: that's Bauer from Marburg?'

Oskar nodded. He was still sitting on the sofa. The scene embarrassed him. He gave a polite, cool smile. 'Good God. How curious. . .'

Anton seized Bauer's hand and shook it. 'Don't you remember? We were in the History Department together.'

He said his and Oskar's names.

'No. Well I never,' said Bauer. His blue eyes looked into nothingness. He was still standing there submissively, his hands by his sides. 'Marburg? Wait a minute. Marburg? It's such a long time ago. I'm sorry, you must excuse me, gentlemen, but I really can't recall details. So much has happened since then. Marburg, yes, yes. But since then, well. . . The university, my God. So it's still there. Still the same. Are you still there, then? Apologies for asking you gentlemen so directly. . .'

'Yes, still studying,' said Anton, 'but we'll soon be finished. Thank God. Just another semester or two. We're going on a study trip to Holland. Or rather, he's on a study trip, and I'm just tagging along for the fun of it. He's working on Calvin, you see, and so he's got to go to Holland, to Amsterdam. Important material. Well, you know how it is. I expect you'll laugh at all this stuff now. Must seem silly.'

'No, not at all,' said Bauer, in a calm, modest way. 'It's just I got out of all that. Anyway, I shan't disturb you gentlemen any longer. Would you like to come to dinner now? The captain's waiting.' He cast an amiable, respectful look at Anton for a moment, a smile across his wide mouth, and dimples appeared in his pockmarked cheeks. His pert, upturned nose protruded awkwardly from his face. Like a clown's, thought Anton. Then he bowed low, more to Oskar than to Anton, and disappeared, soft and noiseless in his white canvas shoes.

Anton poured some water into the basin and washed his hands; Oskar did the same. 'Bauer from Marburg. Can hardly believe it. Here on the *Adelaide*.' Anton shook his large, round head. 'Penny for your thoughts? You haven't said anything.'

'I find the whole thing embarrassing. Frankly.'

'Oh please. Embarrassing? Oskar, what nonsense. It's nice, isn't it, to see the chap again? I feel sorry for him. Don't quite know why.'

'Just don't be too familiar. He's the steward. What would be best would be if no one on board realised that we knew him.'

'Oh Oskar, that's rather shabby.'

'We don't have any towels either,' said Oskar, holding his wet hands reproachfully in the air. He pressed the bell.

There was a knock and the steward entered, soft and noiseless.

'There aren't any hand towels,' said Oskar. He shot a sharp, supercilious look at Bauer. That's Oskar: punctilious to a fault, thought Anton.

'Apologies. I shall bring some immediately.' Bauer's blue eyes were guilt-stricken and helpless. He disappeared and came straight back, two towels over his arm. While Oskar and Anton dried their hands, he said quietly: 'Won't you come to dinner, gentlemen? The captain is waiting.'

'Right you are,' said Oskar. 'Lead on.'

Bauer opened the door for them and let them go first, bowing again slightly. You don't have to be quite so obsequious, thought Anton. He felt awkward for Bauer.

They made their way through the ship, along the corridors, past cabins, past the galley, where the cook stood, dressed in white. They looked into the engine room and could hear the rattling and squeaking of the crane lowering goods into the ship's hold. The ship was black, and lay in the black night, on the black water. Some light fell from the cabins onto the quay and into the smooth water. It was very quiet in the harbour now. The water lapped against the quay wall. The men on the *Adelaide* were the only ones moving about, and their cries sounded through the night. Erich and Hans had finished their close inspection of the ship now; they had looked into the cabins, into the hold; they had watched Oskar and Anton in their cabin and seen the steward arrive in his white jacket, he had two towels over his arm, and they had seen the captain on the bridge and heard his loud, raw voice. My God, the man could scold and curse. They could not see him any more, he was sitting in the dining room, waiting to have supper with Oskar and Anton. His thuggish, hairy hands lay on the table, fiddling irritably with a knife and fork. Damn these passengers! Well, at least they were getting off at Rotterdam.

Erich and Hans were sitting on a coil of rope. For a long time they said nothing. It was so lovely, dusk. The sky was heavy and opaque. No moon. The night wrapped itself round them. Things were quietening down now on the *Adelaide*, too. The fat hulks of the ships lay there round and mute. The boys breathed in the tart, woody smell of the squat warehouses. They had soaked up the warmth of the sun which beat down on them all day, and were now breathing it out again. A cat, with a quiet miaow, circled the building, its legs splayed, its body arched.

Then Erich said timidly: 'Can we go home now, at least?'

Hans looked with disdain into the water. After a while, he chuckled: 'Luise's bound to be asleep now. What a drag.'

'Oh, she'll have been asleep for ages. Wonder what time it is. Must be very late.'

'Luise's actually pretty decent, isn't she?' asked Hans.

'Yes, pretty decent.'

'But she is a girl.'

'Yes.'

'She's much nicer than Fifi, for example.'

'Oh yes, Fifi's silly. She sometimes has that stupid laugh.'

'But Luise doesn't.'

'No, Luise doesn't. She's decent.'

Hans yawned. 'Well, we'd better get going now, back home. You're tired.'

They dawdled through the harbour. Erich had to check his pace. He would have loved to rush home like a shot, but he knew he couldn't. He sauntered along next to Hans, carelessly. Hans stopped again outside the Astoria. 'Should go in, really.' The sound of music and raised voices reached them from the beer garden. The porter came up to them. 'It's not something for the likes of you. Go on, off to bed.' Hans turned and looked behind him. There was no one there. 'Who was he talking to?'

'Calvin?' asked the captain. He was trying to be interested. His eyes looked across at Oskar with blunt courtesy, and a couple of creases appeared on his plain, short forehead from the strain. 'Did he live in Holland, then? My God. . . you never really hear about people like him.'

'No, he was Swiss,' explained Oskar, with a dignified air. 'But, as you know, Dutch Protestantism took on Calvinistic forms.'

'Protestantism? News to me. Well, well. Very interesting. So you're going to the spot where this Protestantism. . .'

'No, I'm not researching Protestantism. I'm interested in the relationship between Calvinism and the ethics of commerce. . .'

'I'm sorry. You've lost me. Blood and sand!' Captain Martens leaned back and forced a laugh. His fat, red, hairy hands lay on the table, holding his knife and fork bolt upright. Horrendous, prattling on with this show-off. What was the point? Why were the ship-owners always making things difficult? This is the last time I take passengers. . .

'Yes, the relationship between Calvinism and Dutch commercial ethics in the sixteenth and seventeenth centuries. I.e. . . .'

Anton could not stand it any longer. 'This really is of no interest to Captain Martens,' he said. 'Stop torturing him with this stuff.' How embarrassing this conversation must be for Bauer, too, who stood stock-still, in silence, next to the table, or walked quietly back and forth with dishes and plates. He gave a painful smile, and sometimes looked uneasily at the captain with his soft, blue, girl-like eyes. His pockmarked skin blushed. The captain, likewise, kept looking across at Bauer during the meal with a peculiarly menacing gaze.

Then suddenly the dog, which was sitting next to the captain on the sofa, laid its paw on its master's broad thigh. It was a fat, repulsive creature. A white, short-haired terrier with a couple of black patches and evil little eyes. It started to whine quietly, looking first at the captain's plate, at the piece of meat which lay there red and juicy, then at the captain's red, blue-veined face.

'Oh, you'd like something, too, would you? Is little Nelly hungry?'

Nelly's whining got louder, and it fawningly raised its head.

'Forgot to again,' said the captain, and cast a threatening look at Bauer. 'What were you thinking?' He patted the dog's fat body a couple of times. 'That an animal like this doesn't need to be looked after? The dog, as part of the senior crew, is your superior, you bugger. Got it?'

Bauer crumpled. He looked down, to one side. 'Yes, Captain,' he breathed.

'Right, get going! Fill his bowl and bring it here. What do you look like?' Captain Martens stood up. He walked very close to Bauer and slowly looked him up and down. 'Stand up.' Bauer stood up straight. 'Look at me.' Bauer obeyed, with deeply submissive, unhappy eyes. They looked at each other for a moment in silence. Captain Martens was breathing heavily. 'Now go, fetch the bowl,' he then said, and sat back down. Bauer slipped limply from the room.

'Nelly. A girl, then?' said Oskar, trying to change the subject.

'Wrong. A boy,' laughed Captain Martens. He raised the dog up by its forelegs to show that he was not a girl. 'I can't remember myself why he's called Nelly, but he's a boy all right. Or are you a little girl? Or a little girly boy, my chubby little moppet?' He petted the dog again, gently squeezing its chest. The dog snorted and grunted with delight.

'Do you realise,' said Anton, 'we know Bauer, the steward, from before.'

'Really?' said Captain Martens. Oskar looked reproachfully at Anton. He really should keep his mouth shut.

'He used to be a student in Marburg,' said Anton. 'He's certainly seen better days. Makes you feel sorry for him, doesn't it, when. . .'

'Ha, not a bit of it. You have to keep the boy in line. Such a slovenly lad. But I'll fix him. He knows now about following orders properly. Yes, yes, I know, this isn't all he's seen of the world. There's all kinds of things in his past. I got that out of him. Had to tell me. Come on, Bauer, I say.

Let's have it, fire away, no secrets—and he has to talk, whether he likes it or not. You know, the lad just has no energy. He's soft. Used to be in some low-grade music-hall show once. Did songs, funny songs. Did you know that?'

'No,' said Anton. 'I feel really sorry for him.'

'Sorry? Why? He's got it good here. Wouldn't want it any different. This is what he wants. . . What do you know, anyway?'

Bauer came back in with the bowl and the dog food. He put the bowl on the floor and called: 'Nelly.' Captain Martens gently shoved Nelly off the sofa. 'Go on, eat.' Nelly stood on the carpet and barked excitedly at Bauer for a while before turning to the food, snarling.

'Fritz,' said Captain Martens. 'You could sing us one of your songs. The gentlemen would like to hear you.'

'Oh no,' said Bauer in great alarm, stepping back a little. 'Not now.'

'Yes, now. Don't be coy, lad. Show us what you can do.'

'Captain, not now, please.' Bauer wrung his hands and looked at him with pleading eyes.

'You will sing if I order you to. Bring me the squeeze-box.'

'Captain, please no, not in front of the gentlemen. They know me. We used to. . . Please don't make fun of me.'

'Come on, hop to it, go fetch the squeeze-box. I'll play along. A song and dance from you. You're in for the surprise of your lives, gentlemen. . .'

'If Herr Bauer isn't in the mood, we're quite happy to do without. You can see he doesn't want to,' said Anton. Oskar looked in embarrassment at his plate.

'Herr Bauer doesn't want to? We'll see about that. It isn't a question of whether Herr Bauer wants to or not. Will you bring that thing here?'

Bauer fetched the accordion and said quietly: 'Please, Captain. Don't do it.'

The captain laughed. 'Oh no, I shall, I shall. What's it to be first? Wild Annie of Bilbao? Come on, let's sing that. Listen to this, learned gentlemen.'

And he began to play.

Bauer looked at Anton. His face said: I'm sorry, but there's nothing I can do. I have to. And I want to, too. He wants me to, and I want to: it's both degradation and desire. His eyes were soft and sad and tortured and sensual. And he put his hands on his hips and began to sway in time to the music. He looked again at Anton and Oskar.

'No,' he cried. 'This is horrible. You can't do this to me. It's not on.' And he ran out.

Captain Martens sat there, louring and speechless. He put the accordion to one side. All that could be heard was Nelly noisily licking his bowl.

Oskar stood up. 'Excuse me, we must go.'

Anton asked: 'What time does the steamer leave?'

Captain Martens forced a friendly smile. 'At twelve. So you still have two and a half hours.'

'What shall we do? How about looking around the harbour again?'

'Yes, do that. And go for a walk along the waterfront. It gets quite interesting in the evening. The Astoria, for example.'

'All right, we'll take a look.'

When they were outside in the corridor Oskar simply said: 'Disgusting. Ugh. . .'

They planned to go for a short walk. Who knows when they might come to this town again? They went to the cabin to fetch their hats and coats. Oskar went straight onto the quay, but Anton needed to go to the toilet. The shock of it all had affected his stomach. As he was heading outside again along the corridor, he passed the galley. There, in the bright white light of the little room, sat the steward, his head laid on his arm. His shoulders twitched. Anton went in.

'Don't take it too much to heart, Herr Bauer.'

Bauer looked up. Silent tears rolled down his pockmarked cheeks from his blue, girl-like eyes.

'He's so horrible to me. Humiliating me in front of you like that!'

'Why does he do it?'

'He wants to torture me. He enjoys it. He's always after me. He's ruined me.'

'But why? Why?'

Bauer smiled a sombre, embarrassed smile. 'Yes, it's certainly a strange kind of love. But you see, when you're all alone, at sea, and can't take women with you, you're bound to go a bit strange, resort to such things.'

'Oh,' said Anton glumly.

'It's a need, to torture me, he enjoys it, it drives him wild. Oh, you should see him. . .'

'Yes, but why do you let him? Leave.'

'Yes, I know, I should leave,' said Bauer. 'But finding another job isn't easy either. And then. . . You get so discouraged. . . You don't know what to do. So you just stay right where you are.'

'Herr Bauer, leave. Whatever happens. Better no job at all, I should think, than one like this.'

'Yes, you're right, I should try. But I'll only drift back again.' Bauer looked away in embarrassment.

'It's entirely up to *you*, Herr Bauer,' cried Anton.

'I know,' said Bauer. His tired blue eyes fell on the doorway. Nelly, the dog, was suddenly standing there.

'There, there, you see,' cried Bauer. 'He's sniffing after me again already. It's that vile, filthy soul of his, hidden in that animal.'

Nelly slowly went up to Bauer, with a low snarl and wild, flashing eyes. The hackles rose on its podgy back.

'Go away, you brute,' cried Bauer. 'You horrible lump.'

Nelly's bark grew louder and louder, shorter and harder.

'Here we go again,' called Bauer with a pitiful look towards Anton. 'The beast is always attacking me, like it's trying to eat me. Go away, you fiend. . . It's jealous, too. Leave me in peace.' But Nelly was not about to, the small, round, hard body lunged at Bauer with increasing violence, snapping furiously at his face, tearing at his clothes. Bauer pushed the dog away with his hands and his feet, tumbling back towards the table till he was leaning backward over the edge. Then his hand hit against a meat cleaver which was lying on the table. Nelly leaped up again, and this time did not just catch Bauer's trousers, but bit firmly into his thigh. The dog hung onto his leg, thrashing about and snarling greedily. Bauer screamed with pain. The whole of his pockmarked face went red, right up to the roots of his soft, blond curls. Suddenly he seized the cleaver and brought it down, with a crack, on the dog's head. Nelly flopped to the floor and was at once silent.

'Oh, good Lord,' said Bauer, dropping the meat cleaver.

Nelly lay motionless, legs splayed apart, eyes twisted and staring.

'I think he's had it,' said Anton.

Bauer smiled, helpless and confused. The pretty dimples appeared in his cheeks.

The cook materialised in the doorway. With a white smock and a white hat. He had to duck slightly in order to get through the door with his white hat. Bauer stared at him, aghast.

'Don't look so daft,' said the cook. 'Oh, good evening, sir. Are you one of our two passengers?'

'Yes,' said Anton, and glanced at the dog.

'Look at that impudent mutt. Lying right in the middle of the galley.' He kicked it with his foot.

'He's asleep,' said Bauer, quickly picking him up. Nelly's head hung limply down, swinging. The legs were stiff. 'I'll take him to his basket.'

'Good God, you're friendly all of sudden!' said the cook, shaking his head.

Bauer disappeared with the dog. Anton followed him.

Bauer leaned over the railing and dropped the body of the dog into the water. There was a splash.

'What shall I do now?' said Bauer. 'He'll flog me to death when he finds out.'

'You need to leave before he notices,' said Anton.

'Yes, I must,' said Bauer, quite apathetic. 'And you won't say anything?'

'No,' said Anton.

'Thank you,' said Bauer. 'Excuse me.' He disappeared quietly along the dark corridor in his canvas shoes. The night was still and black, and Anton looked momentarily into the water where the body of the dog was now floating. He could not make it out. Maybe it had already sunk. The fat little animal was now filling up with water.

'Where have you been?' said Oskar. Anton told him everything. They walked along the quay.

'That captain is a sadist,' said Oskar.

'My worry is that Bauer likes being tortured by him,' said Anton unhappily.

'I can't believe that.'

'It's true. He obviously suffers terribly, but he enjoys it, too. That's what's so frightful. I told him he needs to leave, and he has to now the dog's dead. But do you think he will?'

'I've no idea, and I don't want to hear any more about it.'

They were nearing the harbour exit. They could already hear the town. In the sky, the dull gleam of the moon appeared behind thin, grey wisps of cloud, with thicker, darker clouds round it. The moonlight flowed around the grey warehouses over the quay wall into the harbour basin, over the ships' masts, ropes and funnels. Tired and feeble, it slid over the shiny, almost motionless water. As they walked past the white pleasure steamer Berta and Karl had been on earlier, and which now lay there completely dead, the helmsman was just crossing the gangplank onto dry land. He was going to the Astoria. He walked along the gangplank with firm steps, the wood thudding under his heels.

The two friends carried on for a time, walking along the waterfront, until they decided to go to the Astoria. They strolled along the harbour road, past the customs house, past the public-houses, past all the men and girls walking back and forth, they went as far as the ramparts and saw the moat and the windmill and the railway bridge. A train slipped past on the embankment, its lights flying through the water in the moat. As they passed the sausage-stand, a brief wave of nausea came over Anton. He couldn't help thinking about the dog. Its body floated calmly away, swollen up with harbour water. The moon shone dully on its white fur. They leaned on the railings which ran round the moat and looked at the water for a while in silence. The swan was asleep in front of its little house, its head under its wing. A rotten old boat lay pegged fast to the bank. The dark sails of the mill, like a bat's wings, rose up out of the trees into the grey moonlight.

Anton suddenly laughed to himself. 'Fancy talking to him about Calvin.'

'All right, that's enough,' said Oskar. 'Come on, let's go back to the road.' And they walked back to the harbour road, they had already noticed the Astoria, covered in lights and colour posters, and now they stood before it again.

'Shall we?' asked Anton.

'It'll just be something daft,' said Oskar.

'Could be fun,' said Anton. 'And we are here. . .'

The porter stretched out his arms: 'Gentlemen, please. The main act, tonight's star turn, is still to come. The fight between Dieckmann and Alvaroz.' The porter went over to the box office and knocked on the window: 'Two, please.' The curtain went back and the window opened. The young woman looked at the two friends with a tired, cool gaze. The carefully set waves in her hair shone a poisonous yellow. In front of her lay small piles of coins. She was just sorting the takings.

'We have to now,' said Oskar.

As they walked through the archway, soft, sweet, slow-moving dance music floated out towards them, and when they reached the beer garden they saw a couple dancing on the shell-like vaulted stage. It was Nita and Fred. Nita's silver sequin dress glittered. Fred wore a black tailcoat and a top hat. Oskar and Anton did what everyone here did, they sat at a table under the trees and ordered a glass of beer.

Anton was still not completely there. He could not help thinking about Bauer. Bauer had such a nice face. What was he going to do now?

People sat under the trees and the music played, the leaves on the trees hardly moved, the jazz band sat under a canopy, and lots of men were smoking, and the smoke rose gently into the treetops, and over there a couple was dancing, the girl was blonde and had an average face, a cheeky nose and cheeky eyes, but she was quite sweet, and her dress glittered. Her partner wore his top hat at an angle on his narrow, pale forehead, and his eyes stared fixedly into the audience as he threw his limbs around in time to the music.

Not far from Oskar and Anton sat Karl and Berta. Karl had just eaten a sausage and a potato salad, and was now having a good slug of beer. Berta, her head propped on her hand, was looking indifferently at the stage.

'I've seen this kind of thing a hundred times before,' she said. Then she saw the helmsman. He was looking at her quite openly, in fact he'd turned himself towards her slightly in his chair and gave her a nod, a wink. He knew no shame, this chap. This really was too much! Berta looked at the stage. He mustn't think she was an easy catch. She hadn't been that sort for a long time.

Fred stepped behind Nita and took her by the hands. Their bodies were aligned one behind the other, making the exact same movements, raising their legs, bending to the side, bending forward and back.

'He doesn't care about you at all,' whispered Fred, his white face motionless. His eyes stared coldly at the audience.

Nita laughed quietly. Mockingly, she pursed her lips. 'And? Everything's all right, then.'

'Do you think the only reason I'm here is to dance with you? I shall leave you, you know, simple as that.'

'What will you do without me?'

'I'll go back to being a magician.'

'Oh Freddie, be nice. Quiet now. People are looking. . .'

'So what? I'm fed up with. . .'

The music ended with a long, full chord. Nita and Fred froze for a few moments in an awkward position. Then they trotted off the stage. Through a little door. Scattered applause. Hands clapped wearily. Hopping around like that was all very well, but, good God, only as an interlude to something better. Nita and Fred trotted back on and gave an exaggerated bow, with fixed smiles. They came on again, but no one was clapping any more. They spread out their arms as if to say: now that wasn't so hard, don't be like that.

'Oh, good grief,' thought Anton.

The band started up again, the music loud and crisp. It was time for dancing now. The first to brave the dance floor was a sailor with his girl. He swayed smoothly back and forth across the wooden floor. His wide trousers swung from side to side. The girl smiled coyly at the audience. She didn't want to be the first to dance. Was no one else coming? Everyone's sitting there so quietly. Here they were, all alone on this great dance floor, with everyone looking at them. The people were calmly sitting under the trees, the lights casting a gentle glow among the green leaves, and the leaves hanging motionless, it was as if, for a few moments, all the people were in a dream world, as if they were asleep. . . Cigar smoke rose soft and straight into the sky, curling round the leaves and disappearing into the night. Then came a gentle breeze, ruffling the tops of the trees, sweeping round the people, fluttering the coloured tablecloths slightly, and people started to move again: someone stood up here, a bow over there, people looked for a suitable partner, and found one; couples went up the little wooden steps onto the dance floor, more and more until they were crowding, shoving, pushing their way through. Even two negroes came up with their girls, dancing with short, hard thrusts through the dense rows.

'That's funny, I thought there was supposed to be wrestling, now it's all variety acts and dancing,' said Anton. They were sharing their table with a fat man, his hat on the back of his head, his hands folded across his stomach, a cigar hanging from his mouth, well fed and comfortable, brooding to himself. Beside him a beer glass and a programme. To begin with he did not hear when Anton asked: 'Excuse me, isn't there any wrestling?' Anton asked again. Then he woke up. His gaze came from far away. He sat up slightly, rising up dreamily as if from out of thick, sluggish waters. 'What? Yes, but the bouts are spread out. Then there's some dancing, and then they do something on the stage. It's all a bit of a mess, but the wrestling's the main thing.' He laid a fat finger on the programme: 'You need to look here. Where were we? Oh yes. Nita and Fred. Dance couple, we've just had them, then it's general dancing. Yep, there we are you see. . . Then it's the psychic prodigy. What's that, do you think? A boy wonder. Yes, and then, look. . . Good gracious'—he sat up properly and pushed his hat even further back—'then it's Dieckmann and Alvaroz, phenomenal they are, the best wrestlers around, that's why I'm sitting here, you know, but the other stuff's good, too, the whole evening is—the air, these warm September evenings—oh, it's all over so quick, then it's October, and it's all gone. But enough of that: sit here, what, enjoy a few drinks and watch the show.' And he took a long draught from his beer glass and leaned back again, dreamily sinking down again into the dark, sluggish waters, floating slowly away in the broad, viscous tide.

Anton thought: a river god, coming to the surface with his wide, bubbling mouth, the slimy water running off him, then sinking back again. Anton said: 'Thank you. I think the porter mentioned those two wrestlers.' 'Alvaroz, yes, he said something like that,' said Oskar. 'It's really quite ridiculous, us sitting here,' he added.

Meanwhile, the helmsman went straight up to Berta's table and bowed. Berta looked at her husband. The helmsman turned to Karl: 'May I?'

Karl said: 'Oh yes, please do. . .'

Berta said: 'I don't think I'll dance.'

Karl said: 'Don't be like that. My wife—this *is* my wife, ha, ha, but that's by the by—really loves dancing, but it's not my thing. Please.'

Berta got up hesitantly: 'If you're sure. . . But I'm really not that bothered at the moment.' Karl shook his head in annoyance. Honestly, what kind of behaviour was that?

The foxtrot had come to an end, the dancers separated, standing there in a moment of indecision. The band leader stepped towards the edge of where the band sat and wearily looked over at them with caution. The faces of the musicians glistened just as dull and indifferent. You could see the bass fiddle, dark and brown, the propped-up lid of the piano gleaming smooth and black.

Everyone had bowed their heads to the band leader. Then they clapped. The band leader turned round and went back, like a toy figure in a weather house. On we go then. Never-ending. Tonight, tomorrow, the day after. One of these days I'm going to suddenly puke, thought the band leader.

But you could not hear it in the music when it came, it was sensual and inviting, a warm, viscous waltz. The couples twirled slowly.

The helmsman pressed Berta against him, sure of victory: 'I've got you again, then.' For a few moments Berta, her head tipped back, enjoyed the firm pressure of his arm, the broad chest, the thick, sturdy neck, the provocative stubble chin, but then all of a sudden she said drily: 'You've got a nerve. Be a bit more careful. You can't do anything you like with me, you know.'

'Oh, but he's so stupid,' said the helmsman.

'He's a really good chap. Leave him alone. He's more respectable than you.'

'That's it for this evening, then, is it?'

'Yes,' she said.

A girl called over to the helmsman, laughing. 'Evening, Kalli.'

'She's laughing at you, you know her, then.' The helmsman looked away from the girl. 'I don't know her at all. A case of mistaken identity. Her, I ask you.'

'You *do* know her. And I can imagine how.'

A negro was dancing next to them. His darkly glistening face was right next to Berta. He looked at her. The blue-brown skin, the tight waves of hair, such a pervasive smell, thought Berta. Grinning, the negro parted his thick lips—oh, what strong teeth, what sparkling eyes. Berta stared into his face, at the succulent mouth, the glistening eyes.

'Oh I see, a negro, that's what you'd really like, is it?' said the helmsman.

Berta stared at him. 'Yes,' she managed, hoarsely. The helmsman started slightly. What was all this about? She was voracious, insatiable.

At that moment Jonny looked at his watch. It lay on his hairy arm over a tattoo. It was time. He finished his beer and made his way through the tables, puffing on a cigar. Verandas enclosed the stage area. Jonny went under one and through a door. He came into a small courtyard. There, in the middle, stood a broad, leafy elm. One side of the courtyard formed the back wall of the stage, a little set of steps leading directly up onto it. On the other side were some low, wooden shacks in which the performers had their rooms. In the corners stood bits of apparatus, balls, boxes, a trapeze, with a couple of pieces of scenery leaning against the walls: a Rhine landscape depicting Stolzenfels Castle, a room in a palace, an Oriental pillared hall.

On a bench under the elm sat the announcer. His otherwise sharp, tense face was grey and slack; he stared at the Rhine landscape, and past it, with a look of concern. In one corner a small boy was playing with a dachshund. He wore a white sailor suit and was gently scolding the dachshund in a bright, quiet voice.

'I'm going to get Hein Dieckmann ready. It's time,' said Jonny. 'It always takes an age.'

'He's going soft,' said the announcer. 'He needs to get rid of those rolls of fat.'

'I massage him every day but, well, if he will eat like a horse. . .'

'How old is he then?'

'Thirty-five.'

'Oh, that's all right—anyway—my wife's written to say she's ill. Nephritis. The stupid thing is, I can't go and see her.'

'Bad luck,' said Jonny, snorting through his nose in embarrassment. He looked to one side. 'Who's the little urchin?'

'The hypnotist's son. A "prodigy". The new act. Be on in a minute.'

Jonny shook his head. 'Bloody hell, he's only little.'

'He puts too much of a strain on him,' said the announcer. 'I've seen it before. He won't last long.'

'I'm amazed you have these things standing outside.' Jonny pointed at the scenery. 'It's all very well if the weather's good, but if it rains. . .'

'They can stand it. The rain's spoiled them all already anyway. If you look closely, you can see the streaks. In some places whole sections have been washed away. They still look all right from a distance, though. Just don't get too close. Anyway, as I was saying. My wife's in hospital, all alone, and the nurse has written to. . .'

'Sorry, I need to see to Hein. Haven't much time.' Jonny walked off. He stopped by the boy, bent down and slapped the little dog's body with his great fat hand. 'Won't he do what he's told?'

The child raised his pale face and looked at him timidly with his blue eyes. 'He won't sit up and beg.'

'A few good whacks, then he'll do it.' Jonny gave an easy laugh and went on. The dance was over. The helmsman and Berta had made up. He had a day off on Thursday, she was going to come to his place in the afternoon, but he mustn't be so presumptuous. She expected courtesy. But of course. He knew about distinctions. She was something quite special compared to the other girls around. Yes, Karl was in the office till eight, poor thing—so it was all quite easy. Right, that was enough for this evening, there was no point in trying on anything here. They could have said that straight off, but when people are mad about each other, they always act stupidly. Farewell, then. See you Thursday, 54 Hafenstrasse, don't forget. 'Let go. He's looking.'

As Berta sat down again, Karl asked: 'Do you know that man? You seemed very friendly. . .'

'That was the helmsman from the steamer. I danced with him this afternoon. Quite barmy.'

'You looked at him strangely.'

'Oh, don't start. What's next?'

'A child prodigy, it says.'

The announcer had lifted the boy onto his knee. He reminded him of his own son. He was all alone at home now, without his mother. If only there were a night train, then he could travel late at night and would be back by tomorrow evening.

'The man said I should give him a good beating, and then he'll obey. But I'm not going to do that. There are other ways of teaching him.' The little brown dachshund sat in front of them, looking at his master with his wily little eyes, his head cocked.

'Why are you teaching him all this stuff, Addi? You don't need to. Just play with him.'

'I do play with him, but I want to teach him things, too. Dogs can do such wonderful tricks. I want him to walk on his front feet and jump through a hoop and sit at a table and eat like a real person. I'm having a costume made for him.'

'But why, Addi? There's no need to torment him like that. You wouldn't fret so much yourself, then, either.'

'No, I'm going to teach him things. Quickly, too. There isn't much time.' Troubled, the announcer studied the unhappy face of his little friend. He looked really preoccupied.

'What's the matter? What's all this about?'

Addi put his arm round the announcer's neck and whispered in his ear: 'Promise you won't tell Papa?'

'No, of course not. What is it?'

'When I've trained him properly, I'm going to leave Papa, I'm going to run away in secret, and I'm going to do performances on my own with Fips, and we'll earn our own money, lots of it, and. . .'

His father stood before them. 'Come on, Addi. Time to get ready.'

Addi quickly slid off the announcer's knees.

'Brush your hair,' said the solid, red-cheeked man as he gave Addi the once-over. 'Shirt clean? No, course not. You shouldn't be digging in the sand in your sailor suit just before you go on.'

'I was playing with Fips.'

'Oh, always that filthy mutt. We're getting rid of him. That's the last time you get dirty.' He turned to the announcer: 'That's the thing when they haven't got a mother. I have to be both parents in one. Hands,' he commanded. 'Dirty, always dirty. Wash them, quick. Why can't you do these things for yourself?' Addi ran into the shack. 'Come straight back,' his father called after him.

'Doing an act with a child is the hardest thing, I can tell you. You can rely on adults. Children are unpredictable. You probably think I'm too strict. But I'm just licking him into shape. Strict discipline: that's the answer.'

'Maybe it's not right for children as young as that to be on the stage,' said the announcer quietly.

'Nonsense,' said Addi's father. 'They work best. It's the women, you see, the emotion. . .'

'But what you're doing to the boy, it could harm him.'

'Rubbish. I've spoken to the experts, and they said that as long as I'm careful and don't do it too often. . .'

'But you're on here every night, for two weeks.'

'Yes, *here*, that's an exception. We're taking a break afterwards.'

Addi came back. A bell sounded, and the announcer went, his mind troubled, up the wooden steps onto the stage area to introduce them. As he opened the door and stepped into the light he drew himself up, a propitious smile on his face, and rubbed his hands. 'And now, ladies and gentlemen, a delightful surprise, a scene between father and son which will have you. . .'

'You're drunk,' cried Jonny, stepping right up close to Hein Dieckmann. He could smell brandy. 'Christ, you are stupid. Just before going on?' Hein had been lying on the chaise longue. Jonny had switched on the light and shaken him awake—thank God he was changed and ready—and Hein had stood up, swaying oddly and muttering, the idiot, and now he was standing in front of Jonny, and Jonny had taken off his robe, and Hein was supposed to prove he was ready. Then this.

'You haven't done this since Kassel. I gave you a good enough hiding then, you bastard. Now you're doing it all over again.' Jonny was beside himself. He was close to tears. 'Now you've screwed up everything, for both of us.'

'I know, you're right,' whimpered Hein Dieckmann, his face drained, and looked desperately out of the open window at a bush which stood by a wall. 'But there's no need to be rude. It doesn't matter, anyway. This fat old lump is past it. Look at it all, sagging, wobbling,' he moaned, gripping the rolls of fat on his belly. 'Used to be hard and smooth and tight once, Jonny.'

'You can get it back.' Jonny glowered, looking Hein up and down. 'Pull yourself together. Exercise properly, no over-eating, pay attention to me, and it'll all be fine, you'll see.'

'No, it's all over,' bleated Hein, and tried to walk to the window as straight as he could, but was still lurching slightly. 'It's all over.' He looked outside. At the blank walls. 'It's all right for the moment, but it'll soon be all over. Bang, and there I'll be, lying on the floor, and them all screaming and whistling. I can't listen to that. And him, he'll be standing there, all fancy grand, with them cheering and clapping, and he'll be laughing, and I'll just be lying there, on the floor. I can't do it.'

'Who? Who'll be standing there?' asked Jonny. 'Who are you jabbering on about, man?' Jonny had pressed Hein's arms by his sides and was looking blankly at his broad, beefy back. Hein turned round. He bent down mysteriously towards Jonny, his face came right up to Jonny's.

'I've seen him,' he whispered. 'I've seen him. That's it, you see. He's so young, and gorgeous, bleeding gorgeous.'

'Who, for God's sake?'

'This Alvaroz, or whatever he's called. Bleeding gorgeous,' moaned Hein.

'Oh, I see,' said Jonny. 'It's got you again. Another crush, is it?'

'He's phenomenal,' said Hein. 'You'd say so, too.'

'Where did you see him, then? When you all trooped on?'

'No, no. He wasn't there. He didn't take part. Someone like that can do as he pleases. No, later on. I had to go and take a piss, back there in the whatsit. And there he was, with his robe over his shoulder. I knew straight away it was him. I said as much to him while I was having a piss, and he looked down: hello, may I introduce myself, I'm Dieckmann. We'd finally met. And in a place like that. He stood up, turned to me and laughed real nice, and we shook hands. Then his robe fell down. I'm staring like this, crikey, you don't see them like that very often, everything perfect, flawless, and suddenly I felt it, the pain inside, twisting over and over, burning, stabbing. He's so young, and gorgeous. Smooth hair, all slick, black eyes, white teeth, a beautiful laugh, and that body—broad shoulders, brown skin, neat little hips. . . He said he was pleased to meet me, and then that friendly laugh again, and he shook my hand. See you later, he said, and left. Must have wondered why I was gaping at him like that. . .'

'Bollocks,' said Jonny. 'This always happens. You fall for the goon. But what did you get drunk for?'

'He's so gorgeous,' moaned Hein. 'He's so gorgeous and so young, and I'm so old and horrible. I can't bear it. I can't compete against that.'

'Always the same old story,' cursed Jonny. 'Makes me want to puke. I've had enough of this.'

'I wish I wasn't like this. When I see someone like that I just want to crawl inside him, inside his body, have every bit of him for myself, the body, the skin, the hair. I'm just a piece of shit. Ugh! Disgusting!'

'Just pull yourself together. Stop it. What do you look like? Don't be so daft. Stand up straight. Loosen up, do a few exercises. Come on, put your head in some water. Here.'

Jonny pulled him over to the little sink, poured some water into the basin, pushed Hein's head deep into the bowl, rubbed it, poured yet more water over the round head.

Hein came up again, his face glistening and his yellow hair stuck to his forehead: 'I don't want to fight a nice chap like that. We should be friends. I don't want to fight him.'

'Ha, I thought that would come.' Jonny looked at him in despair. 'What now, then, eh? Are you going to go and see him and say, would it be all right if we're not too rough today? We've seen that before. Any chance you might have had, gone. And today of all days, when it really matters. The day when you could've shown people that Hein Dieckmann still has it.'

'Yes,' said Hein, 'I'm going to go and see him. I'll say I'm his friend, and he's got to be my friend, too. He's got to like me, he has to—he has to like me.' The final words sounded almost like a threat. Jonny was going to hold on to him, but when he heard those words he suddenly let go. If the bloke isn't nice to him then everything will be just fine. And why would he want to be friends with such a repulsive old soak? If he isn't nice to him, if he doesn't want to—well, yes— Jonny knew full well how angry Hein could get, and how strong that could make him. Then there would be a great fight, a great victory.

The sound of the band whirled up and down, and then stopped. The little boy in the white sailor suit stood completely lost in the great, illuminated shell of the stage, directed by the gaze of his father, who stood to one side with his arms folded. A hush fell over the audience. Addi made a stiff, jerky little bow, bent over completely so that his thin blond hair hung down, and then stood up straight again.

'Ladies and gentlemen,' came the patter in his bright, chirpy voice. 'My father and I will now perform certain tricks, during which I ask you to remain completely silent. The tricks are not without danger. If you make a noise or call out, I could then wake up and in some circumstances come to harm. Please, do not clap. You may clap when my father has said "the end". Then,' he said, raising a delicate finger with a practised impishness, 'we would be glad to receive your applause.' He bowed once again and stepped back. The audience buzzed, with grins of approval.

'How sweet, and such a tiny boy,' said Berta.

'Abuse is what it is,' murmured Anton. 'That boy should be in bed, asleep. You can see he's quite pale.'

'It's a tough old world,' Oskar observed. The man next to them had floated away across the people and tables, far into the distance, in a smoky dream.

Under a tree stood the negro. He was leaning against the trunk, with his eyes trained on Berta. He was wearing blue trousers, a yellow shirt, a belt round his waist, and his shirt collar was open wide. He smirked. Berta looked quickly away.

The hypnotist had gazed piercingly at Addi for a long time before Addi's eyes closed and he stood there rigid, asleep. He then grabbed him by the legs and swung him round in a circle, stiff as a board, then stood him on his head. 'Stay,' he commanded. The hypnotist stood solidly on the stage, his red face beaming with health and energy. Addi remained standing on his head, feet together, arms by his sides, held by the gaze of his father. Then his father stood him up on his feet again. 'Shh, shh,' he said, his finger to his lips, when some people started clapping. He placed two chairs close to each other and laid Addi, the stiff little board, on top. His neck lay on the back of one chair, his legs on the other, but he did not bend. His father stood him up on his feet once again, took the chairs away and signalled towards the back of the stage. Two bellboys came silently on and set up two poles joined by a rope. His father commanded: 'Walk on the rope,' and slowly, jerkily, his arms stiff by his sides, Addi walked with measured steps over to one of the poles, climbed up a rope ladder, moved stiffly across the rope, his eyes closed, and back again, climbed down, and again stood motionless before his father, who looked in triumph at the audience with an ostentatious wave of his arm. The audience started to clap, but again came the 'shh, shh' from the hypnotist.

'Shame about that spot, and on such lovely skin,' said Hein Dieckmann. He swayed slightly and spread his legs apart. He had his hands in the pockets of his green-striped robe as he stared, his mind clouded, at Alvaroz. The latter was standing in front of the mirror, completely naked save for the dark blue trunks round his loins, he had his hand behind him on his back, trying to reach a spot which sat red and fat on his smooth, brown skin.

Alvaroz turned round: 'Oh, is that you, Herr Dieckmann? I was expecting someone else.' He walked amiably over to Dieckmann, looking at him in surprise, but calmly, with his powerful black eyes. He opened his mouth slightly and smiled, revealing his white teeth, his cheeks, clean shaven, shimmered blue-brown.

Hein Dieckmann's eyes ran uncontrollably over Alvaroz's body—the athletic yet youthfully slim limbs, the brown skin, the firm, bulging muscles, twitching slightly—they slid from the broad shoulders, the prominent, hairy chest, to his navel, his trunks. Alvaroz looked at him for a moment, then to one side. He was no longer smiling, his face locked.

'Well, all of a sudden and here I am. Funny that, isn't it?' said Hein, looking up. 'Don't really know why myself. I just wanted to say that I really, really like you. There's a real bloke for you, I thought, good for him. Could be good friends, if you want. Why? Really don't like the idea of fighting with you. It'd be such a shame. And we don't want that, do we?'

'I'm afraid I don't understand you,' said Alvaroz. 'A bout is a bout, its own thing, it's got nothing to do with us as people.'

'Look, I don't want to fight with you. I don't like fighting with friends, don't like laying them out on the floor. They mean too much for that.'

'Let's see if you can get me on the floor first,' said Alvaroz. 'And anyway: are we friends? We hardly know each other.'

'Of course we're friends!' pleaded Hein Dieckmann. 'Alvaroz, a nice chap like you, of course we're friends!' Hein was becoming quite tearful and Alvaroz could smell the brandy on his breath.

'An old wrestler, and he behaves like this,' he said, cool and impervious, shaking his head a little. 'I don't understand. You've had your hands on lots of men. It's nothing new.'

'Oh, it's always the same, Alvaroz,' moaned Hein Dieckmann. 'I see a fine, strapping lad like you, and I'm gone. I can't fight with them. I can't lay out the nice ones, throw them around. . . I just can't. God, your body is divine!' Dieckmann raised a large, red-haired, fleshy hand and gently, tenderly stroked the wiry curls on Alvaroz's chest, his trembling fingers touched the firm, red-brown nipple.

'Get your hands off,' said Alvaroz, stepping back. 'What's all this? You can touch me all you want later, I can't stop you then, but not now. You'll have no luck with me, I'm afraid. You can't get round me. I'm not what you think.'

'I was only offering you my friendship, Alvaroz,' said Hein Dieckmann meekly, reproving him tenderly. 'I don't want anything from you. I was doing you a favour, suggesting today we don't fight quite so fiercely. After all, we're friends, we've agreed. . .'

'We haven't agreed anything. We fight properly, and that's that. I don't do cheating. Pull yourself together, man. You're making a fool of yourself. What made you think I'd get involved in some dodgy deal? Not so sure of yourself any more or something?'

Alvaroz looked at Hein Dieckmann coldly, full of contempt, and turned back to the mirror. For him the subject was closed. Ugh, disgusting, enough, block it from your mind. He turned his back to him, put his hand over his shoulder, twisting his upper body on those narrow hips. When he reached the spot, squeezing it with two fingers, it burst, and some pus and blood ran out. The room was quiet, there was not even the sound of music, as just at that moment Addi was doing his sleepwalking act in the silent beer garden. Light fell from a bare bulb on the ceiling onto the bare, light-green walls, onto the hard chairs, the table, chiselling out Alvaroz's muscles, firm and sharp, and reflecting in his smooth black hair. Outside the window stood the dully lit wall, and above it, brooding black, the night.

Finally, with a groan, Dieckmann rasped his indignation: 'You're a tyke, do you know that? A mean, ungrateful tyke. I come in here, offering you my friendship, me, Hein Dieckmann, your senior, offering *my* friendship to *you*, a stuck-up prig, a snotty little upstart, still wet behind the ears, and you. . .'

'Oh, thank you, and a fine friendship it is, too, throwing yourself round my neck like some old whore. You're a disgrace,' said Alvaroz over his shoulder, quite cold, still dealing with his spot, which he was dabbing with a towel.

'Thought, you look after the lad, you don't want to hurt him, turn a blind eye,' grunted Hein Dieckmann.

'No need for that, Herr Dieckmann. You're mistaken. I don't need your protection. But you might need it, with all this cheating, and under the cloak of friendship. Well, I guess everyone gets old.'

'What?' screamed Hein Dieckmann, the blood surging into his broad neck, into his great head. 'You don't think I came here, do you, because I'm scared of you, hoping you'd. . .'

'All things are possible. One thing I do know is it's a dirty business. That's the end of it. The end. You'll soon have the chance to show what you can do.'

'Oh, that's low, that is low,' cried Hein Dieckmann, stamping on the floor and raising his fist. 'Drag it all through the dirt, why don't you? I was only being friendly, nice. Just you wait, my lad, I'll show you, I'll show you who Hein

Dieckmann is. You've no idea. I'm going to get you good and proper, you horrible lump, bend those lovely bones of yours till they snap.'

At that, the door opened slightly and Nita, the dancer, peered round. Her sequin dress shimmered in the light.

'What's going on here? A little altercation? Gentlemen, please. Peace be with you. Herr Dieckmann, don't scream like that, we can hear you at the other end of the Astoria. I suppose I can come in. Herr Dieckmann, whatever is the matter? Don't stare at me like that. You could give someone a fright. Herr Dieckmann!'

Alvaroz put down the towel and turned to Dieckmann: 'I think it would be better if you left.'

'Yes, yes, don't you worry, I'm going, lad, no need to throw me out. I'll leave you alone with your little turtle dove. There you are. Coo away to your heart's content. That's it, run your hands all over your handsome prince. But just you wait. When I get my hands on you, there'll be nothing to laugh about. Then we'll see if Hein Dieckmann is past it.' Hein turned round and went, muttering indignantly. The other side of the door, his head on one side, stood Fred, the dancer, listening, his top hat askew on his chalky-white forehead. He went up to Dieckmann with a cold civility and stared at him, smiling. 'What a show-off. You give it to him,' he said quietly, oozing charm.

'He's going to get a surprise. Wait till he gets a taste of Hein Dieckmann,' said Hein, and he staggered along the corridor to his dressing room.

'Poor old Dieckmann. He's man-mad,' giggled Nita.

'Dirty bastard,' said Alvaroz, going to the peg to fetch his robe.

'Stay as you are,' begged Nita.

'You're all after something, aren't you?' said Alvaroz. 'Swarming around like flies. I've had enough.'

'Don't you like me, then?' asked Nita.

'No,' said Alvaroz.

'Oh, let me stay with you,' said Nita quietly. 'I only want to give you a bit of a rub.'

'Stop touching me all the time. Come here, and use the powder puff on the patch on my back.' Nita obeyed. She laid her head on his cool back. 'This Dieckmann,' she said. 'I hope he doesn't do anything to you. I'm a bit scared. He gets so angry, and then he's really strong. You know that.'

'Oh, don't you start,' said Alvaroz and shook her off.

The hypnotist lifted his hand and raised his thick eyebrows meaningfully. 'Your attention, please,' he called into the silent beer garden, his red cheeks gleaming. 'Now for something a little special. Something which I shall only do this evening, an extra turn: the Singing Nightingale. Prepare to be amazed. I ask for your complete silence and attention.'

He turned to Addi: 'Addi, my little nightingale, off you go now, up the tree.' A convulsion ran through Addi's body and he set off again, legs stiff, eyes closed, completely asleep. He walked down from the stage and up to the large beech tree to which his father was pointing. It stood a little to one side of the stage, but not far, and visible to everyone in the garden.

'Up, and up, and up,' called Addi's father in a sing-song voice.

Addi stepped on the roots and up, up, up, stiff and machine-like, with extraordinary speed and confidence, he climbed up the trunk. Didn't he need to cling on? Up, up onto the first branch, up onto the second and higher and higher into the thick crown of the tree, until he was suddenly on the uppermost fork of the trunk, where he sat stiff and motionless.

All heads craned upward, some people had stood up to get a better view. There was the odd laugh in places, in consternation and amusement. That was amazing! The boy climbed up there like a squirrel. What was he doing? They looked in excitement at the motionless boy, whose white suit shone through the leaves against the dense blue sky. The hypnotist cupped his hands to his mouth: 'Now, Addi, my little nightingale, sing, sing, sing!'

For a moment there was complete silence, and then a thin child's voice was raised in song, trembling and uncertain at first, a small flickering flame, then increasingly clear, bright and penetrating, casting notes, silver-pure, into the garden, into the full night sky. And the people below did not make a sound, they were listening, their faces looking up, disconcerted, exhilarated, illuminated with sound, into the tree, into the night sky, watching the silver-grey disc of the moon, slightly dinted, rolling through the clouds, watching the clouds beaming, streaming with light, as they sailed past in the warm, sultry breeze, feeling the gentle flow of the night air, the cool of the song, the still of the moment. Coarser types would shake their heads and murmur, 'What nonsense,' yet they still looked up and listened. Berta had raised her face and sat there as if asleep, for a few moments not thinking about the negro at all, who stood by the tree with his glistening eyes and open mouth, his gaze, too, fixed on the top of the tree. Anton and Oskar listened, the helmsman had propped his head on his hand, looking dreamily at the table top, and the hypnotist stood on the stage, smiling in triumph and moving his hands in time to the song. People were breathing more easily, more gently, as if asleep, their muscles relaxed, and they felt the night pass over them like a tender caress. Slow and heavy, the night grew, ripening towards the deepest calm and silence, the darkest of hours. And a soft, thick breeze blew up, burrowing gently in the trees and bearing Addi's song away over the gardens and houses. Most of the streets lay solitary now, and the ships sat hulking and motionless in the harbour, sails had been folded up, water stood in the harbour basin like tar. Even the *Adelaide* was quiet now, only a few lights were on, and the dull engines pumping, and Captain Martens sat in his cabin, wheezing as he wrote, while the little steward was just getting his things together to leave the ship. The river surged past the town, away under the bridges, the piers standing firm against it and staunching its flow. In a few hours, its back would bear the *Adelaide*. A couple of fishing boats lay at the foot of the tall warehouses which ran into the river, anglers, motionless, holding their rods in the water. There were other fishermen down there, too, hauling their nets out of the moonlit waters, the fish shimmering with oil, twisting their bodies, trying to jump back into the water. The swans in the moat dozed by their little house, their heads tucked under their wings, and out of the marshy water rose a putrid mist. And the toads came to the surface, a sustained gurgling from their wide throats, their crystal eyes staring at the rats which scuttled in and out of the tree roots, squeaking and hissing; a marten ran along, purring quietly, before jumping with a splash into the water and sinking its teeth into an eel.

Thick with leaves, the trees by the ramparts breathed in the air. There was no one on the benches and the windmill rose up on the hill with its batwing sails, the park keeper lay in bed, his rotten boat dreaming by the bank, and in the dark parlour, through which the light of the moon occasionally shone, his pointy straw hat hung among the stuffed birds, the newspaper lay on the table with his spectacles in their case, right by the picture of his robust late wife, which hung over the sofa. The old seamen's widows in the 'Seefahrt' had long ago crawled into their striped feather beds, small and shrivelled up; their windows were open and into their dreams crept the splashing of the little fountain in the courtyard and the squawking of a parrot talking in its sleep.

And Addi sang. He sat stock-still in the branches, his pale face tipped back, arms hanging down by his sides, and he sang out of the darkness of his little body into the darkness of the night, the notes drifting away bright and clear. He sang over the treetops, over the Astoria garden. And not far away from him, only a couple of gardens, a couple of houses and streets lay in between, Herr Berg was playing his flute. He was still standing at the window, and the window was open, and Herr Berg's pale, bony fingers went up and down over the holes in the flute. He held his head slightly to one side, and his soft grey eyes listened to the notes. The notes were steady, gently rising, gently falling, peaceful, not entirely happy, not entirely sad, and yet always somewhat plaintive—a pure, resolute and clear-cut sound. Quietly it drifted out into the night, blown by the wind, melting into the still air.

The two men, still sitting under the pergola, Herr Hennicke and the inspector, could feel it, and sometimes looked up from their table, bathed in the warm light of the paraffin lamp, looked up from the dull, hazy glow, in which the midges danced, and breathed in the peace from above. They were swapping postage stamps, before them lay Herr Hennicke's large stamp album, which was already full of the rarest of stamps, and now Herr Hennicke was looking at a new collection which the inspector had brought along; he peered at the delicate, colourful things through a magnifying glass. He already had that one, but was missing this one, and words such as Cuba, Madagascar, Ceylon and Afghanistan dripped, dream-ridden, into the night.

Did Herr Berg realise he was playing in the house of the dead? He did not. Frau Jacobi had said nothing further to him, she had thought no more about it, until Frau Mahler's distraught face had appeared at her door, lit by the weak glow of the light in the stairwell. She had swiftly gone downstairs with Frau Mahler to sit with her in her hour of need. Herr Berg thus knew nothing, but even if he had known, it would not have alarmed him all that much and he would perhaps not even have interrupted his playing. He was familiar with death, had absorbed it, and even his music, in its gentle way, could express it, knew exactly how to express it. Herr Mahler had quietly fallen asleep surrounded by the silver circles of his flute. He breathed gently, lying still in bed, his arms stiff on the covers. A couple of times he breathed in the warm, scented garden air which streamed in through the open window, the air which many a night had come to him and flowed over his body, then he stopped breathing, quite slowly, his breath became lighter and lighter, his mouth remained open and his face turned pale in the light of the bedside lamp. The two women stood transfixed with horror next to the bed; they had embraced each other in support as they watched the approaching enemy, death. But their expressions became quieter and quieter, calmer, fear continued to disappear, as they saw how softly death overtook the man, how it was really nothing more than quietly falling asleep, silently going away.

'It's actually not that bad,' said Frau Jacobi. 'What I mean is. . .'

'How quiet it all is,' said Frau Mahler. But then she saw the bloodless hand, which suddenly looked quite different from before, and she saw the dreadful rigidity of the face. And she threw herself over the dead man. He had gone completely. What was lying there was something quite different, a strange wax doll, a shell, he had vanished—and would never return.

Frau Jacobi stood to one side, observing, her hands folded across her front. She thought it quite all right for Frau Mahler to behave like this. Good God, she had been so silly herself when her husband had died. But you get over it, she had got over it, and Frau Mahler would get over it too. Funny you can't say that straight away, but you just can't.

She bent over Frau Mahler and patted her on the shoulder: 'I'm so sorry, dear. . . He was such a good man. . . You have a proper cry. Then you'll feel better.' And when, in response, Frau Mahler just sobbed more uncontrollably, she stepped back. You need to be patient. Leave her in peace, and let her cry it out. Can't do anything else. Perhaps I can fetch my sewing and sit with her a while longer. In the parlour, in the light, of course, not in here with the body. Would sewing be all right? Tsk, it won't be ready otherwise, Else's birthday is the day after tomorrow. Undecided, Frau Jacobi looked to the side, at the fruit bowl, piled high with apples, which stood on the sideboard. A sharp, slightly rotten smell from the apples mixed with the smells of the garden and recent death. Through the ceiling and the window, Frau Jacobi could hear the odious sound of Herr Berg's flute. Was it really that unpleasant, that distracting, this music wafting, soft, clear and peaceful, over the rigid form of Herr Mahler? Wasn't this the right music for the dead?

Pat, pat, pat. It was Fips, the little brown dachshund, drawn by the sound of Addi singing. He stopped at the foot of the great beech tree, cocked his head to one side and looked up with faithfully glistening, inquisitive little eyes at his master up in the tree. His long ears pricked and, happy, his smooth, firm, little tail wagged excitedly from side to side. And suddenly the song achieved what Addi, with all his assiduous training, never could: as if drawn up by the tender, bright song, Fips sat on his hind legs, raised his front paws in a graceful curve and begged. He sat there motionless, enthusiastically looking up, his little tail thumping the ground in appreciation.

Some people saw the dog sitting like this with its happy, rascally face; they found it funny, pointed at the animal and burst out laughing. Some presumed it was part of the act, probably most of them: Isn't it fantastic? How do they do it? What an amazing performance. How funny! I wasn't expecting that. The mothers thought of their children. Shame they were in bed and couldn't see this.

'This is ridiculous,' said Oskar, shaking his head. 'The whole thing. They don't know what to do either. Make sure you keep an eye on the clock, so we get to the boat in good time.'

'I hope Bauer will have gone by the time we get there,' said Anton.

'If he's sensible.'

The hypnotist was still moving his hands around like a conductor, gazing up, transfigured, with his red-cheeked face, when he heard people laughing, looked down at the ground, saw the little dog, his hands continued to conduct, but the happy smile had disappeared from his face and he stared, dark and with subdued anger, at the animal.

'The boy's got a damned good voice,' said Oskar. 'But to my mind the bit with the dog is quite ridiculous.'

The two of them had stood up to get a better view. 'Look at those wily little eyes,' said Anton, laughing a little.

The hypnotist made a signal to finish the act: 'That's enough now, Addi, my little nightingale, come down, finish, finish your song now.'

Addi fell silent. He immediately stood up in the fork of the tree and climbed down branch by branch, with jerky movements but at amazing speed, slipping lightly down the trunk without any trouble; he was already halfway down when Fips saw him. As soon as the song had stopped, the dog had put its front paws down again, and when he saw Addi he suddenly began to bark, short, sharp and happy. Addi, woken by the barking, immediately opened his eyes, looked around him in dreadful fright, had no idea where he was and stared, with a deathly-pale expression, at the tree, at the garden, the people and the lights, his hands let go of the branch, he faltered. . .

The hypnotist leaped from the stage into the garden and under the tree, followed by the announcer, who had been leaning against the wall under the shade of the veranda:

84

'He's falling, catch him, wait. Got you!' And they caught him together in their arms. 'It's all right, nothing to worry about,' said the announcer, bent over Addi's face. 'See? It's me.'

'Where am I?' asked Addi quietly.

'Here, in the beer garden. See? I'm here, and there's your Papa.'

The audience clapped enthusiastically. A brilliant act. The hypnotist held Addi up by the collar, bowed, heels together; he had to push Addi down. 'Bow. Pull yourself together.' Fips stood next to Addi, looking at him and wagging his tail. Next to Fips stood the announcer, his worried gaze fixed on the boy.

The band started up a brisk march and the hypnotist led the boy across the stage to the courtyard behind, where the elm and the bits of scenery stood, and from there into the wooden shack. Addi was sobbing. 'Little crybaby.'

He laid him down on the chaise longue in their dressing room. 'You can lie there and sleep. What else do you want? Look at you, lying there like a pasha.' He laughed, but Addi did not. He sat up straight, wrapped his arms round his body and retched, looking at his father in despair. His face was greenish-white.

'If you wanted to puke, then you should have said so and we could have gone to the toilet. Now it'll go all over the floor again and we'll get into trouble with the manager.' Addi retched and retched, the little dog stood next to the chaise longue and looked at him with a cocked head and a furrowed brow. Addi tried to stand up, but then up it all came and he hung over the edge of the chaise longue.

'You need to pat him on the back. That helps,' said the announcer, who had just come in; when Addi's father did not do so, he did it himself. 'Can't you see this is exploitation?' he cried, when Addi had lain back, exhausted.

'It's that filthy mutt's fault,' said the hypnotist. 'Otherwise it would've all gone smoothly.' And he gave Fips, who was sniffing the floor with his nose, a kick which sent him flying into the corner, whimpering. 'I'm selling you tomorrow, you mongrel, and if I can't sell you, I'll drown you. You see if I don't.'

Addi started to cry again, got up and went towards Fips in the corner. 'Don't hurt Fips. Please, please. Oh, that really hurt him!'

At that, his father grabbed Addi by his sailor collar like a cat and, with a firm sweep of the hand, threw him back onto the chaise longue. 'Stay there.'

Suddenly it came to him, like a light going on. 'Do you think,' he said to the announcer, 'we could do an act with the dog? That would be a nice addition.'

'I really don't think that would be a good idea,' said the announcer, and left the dressing room.

The two swans were asleep in front of their little house, their heads tucked under their wings, and the house floated in the middle of the water, and the water was quite black, thick and dense, one could not see into it at all. There no light anywhere, and the air was close and wrapped around the swans and the house and on the water, and everything was thick, black, total darkness, and there was the feeling that you could only move through the air with difficulty, that it would flow round you, surging, soft and smoky, and prevent you from moving, sliding forward. But you had to cross the moat if you wanted to see anything. I don't want to see anything, thought Luise, I don't want to see what's happening over there, but then it pulled her, and she slid across, floated over the water, she had to see the swans, she couldn't see anything from the bank. It was a miracle, the dull shimmer from the swans' feathers in this blackness, yes, they must be very, very white for them to shimmer grey-white now, and they became brighter and brighter, whiter and whiter, the nearer she came. A squeak came from the bank. Luise wanted to help the swans, she knew what was coming, but she had no hands to hold on with, couldn't move at all—where was she? Lots of little squeaks. Luise knew full well what that was—but would they come across? They couldn't swim. Luise breathed a sigh of relief. She even laughed slightly at the little monsters. But then she got a dreadful shock: they could swim, and they were throwing themselves into the water—splash, splash, splash—she couldn't see them, but could hear them, their little round bodies shooting through the water, propelled by little feet and twitching, thrusting tails. Ah! Thud. One jumped onto the platform round the swans' house, another thud, a third, and snap, snap, snap into the swans, the sharp teeth sinking into their white bodies, waking the birds with a scream, already bitten half to death, stretching their necks out, the shrill, plaintive cries, spreading their wings wide and beating them in terror. A couple of the beasts hang from each swan, biting, sucking hard, shaking and tearing and tugging at the poor creatures, and the blood streaming over their white bodies, into the water, the water spraying, and feathers flying around and falling silently into the moat. And then the swans, too, fall over the edge of the platform into the water, and they are pulled under by the little bloodsuckers, deep down, and disappear.

Luise had been there, fate had put her there, and yet she could do nothing, she slid back and forth but had no hands to help, all she could do was watch, she wanted to scream, opened her mouth, but then she sank under the water, the bloody water, pulled down, gasping for air. . .

And then, then she could suddenly, suddenly scream, gasping, the thick, bloody water in her throat: 'The swans! The swans! The rats!'

Luise stared at her mother. She was standing by her bed. The bedside light was on.

'Oh Mama,' she cried, 'the rats attacked the swans and bit them to death.'

'It was a dream. There aren't any swans, or rats. It was all a dream.'

'The swans in the moat,' said Luise, looking at her mother. How could she explain? Her mother stood there in a long white nightdress. Her hair was in a plait which hung down her back, a funny little tail. She smiled at Luise in a demure, encouraging way: 'Can you see? You were dreaming.'

Luise looked for a long time at her mother's calm, kindly, sombre face, she looked at her familiar room, she looked out of the open window, the tops of the trees stood motionless and dark over the window ledge, she heard the flute playing and the murmur of voices from Herr Hennicke's garden.

'Yes,' she said. 'Oh, it was horrible. Mama, could rats really bite swans to death?'

'Nonsense,' said her mother. 'Those little animals? Swans can defend themselves, you know. They have beaks they can bite with. They'd bite the rats to death.'

'Really? Is that what they'd do? With their great beaks?'

'Of course. Their beaks are really powerful.'

'Why do we have stupid rats anyway?' grumbled Luise, and yawned.

'We just do,' said her mother. 'But they keep them under control, and one day, you'll see, there won't be any left. Right, back to sleep.'

She stroked Luise's damp forehead, saying: 'It was nothing, it was nothing,' switched off the bedside light and went out. But she did not go straight back to bed, she went to the window for a while, to breathe in the mild, scented garden air—a good, deep breath. Luise's screaming had not woken her, she had not been to sleep at all, just lain there with her eyes open.

Herr Berg's flute drew her with a cool, penetrating clarity. She leaned over the window ledge slightly and a gentle, warm breeze blew through her nightdress onto her skin.

'Will you look at that woman up there,' said the inspector, shaking his head, 'at the window, in a nightdress. She's been standing there for quite a while. Hasn't moved a muscle. Wonder what she's thinking?'

Herr Hennicke looked up, a stamp in one hand, the magnifying glass in the other. 'I think she's dreaming. Maybe she's thinking about her late husband. He's been dead two years. Shame she lost him so young. They were quite happy, I think. They often used to stand at the window together, of an evening. She's little Luise's mother, a favourite pupil of mine.'

'Maybe she wants to listen to the flute a bit longer,' supposed the inspector.

'Who knows,' said Herr Hennicke, and turned back to the stamps. He looked through the magnifying glass. 'There's a smoking volcano and a native hut on it,' he said. 'Hm, would it be a fair trade, do you think, if I swap you a Borneo for the Jamaica? Honestly now.'

'Take them, you pesky blighter,' growled the inspector. 'You're so pig-headed, you do what you want anyway. It's time I went.' He buttoned his jacket and his stiff collar, and listened to the sound of the flute a final time. With a careful hand, Herr Hennicke delicately stuck the Jamaican stamp into his album, closed it, took the lamp from the table, and they walked through the garden and into the cellar. In the laundry room they had to duck slightly to get past the washing which hung there on lines. It hit them in the face, cool and damp. 'Careful with the lamp,' warned the inspector. But a piece of washing had already slapped gently against the glass, and it went out. 'Childish, careless,' murmured the inspector.

'No harm done,' said Herr Hennicke. 'We don't need it now anyway.'

'But the fire risk,' said the inspector.

'Oh, the washing's wet,' said Herr Hennicke.

In the kitchen sat Meta, the serving girl, still up, writing a letter. She was writing to Otto, asking why he didn't come any more. Oh, it was all over now anyway.

Herr Hennicke and the inspector said their goodbyes at the cellar door. 'Good night, old chap.'

'Good night.'

'If it's all right by you, I'll come again tomorrow,' said the inspector, casting a slightly hesitant and wary look through his spectacles.

'Of course. You can always come.'

'Say, won't you, if I bore you, or disturb. . .'

'That's enough of that,' said Herr Hennicke, giving the inspector a friendly cuff. 'Silly ass.'

The inspector looked at Herr Hennicke with gratitude. 'All right, I'll come.' He again shook his hand. 'Good night.'

'Good night.' The door bell tinkled and the inspector, grave and stiff, walked away, through the empty streets, past the front gardens, under the street lamps, towards the customs house, which lay wine-red and silent, with darkened windows, opposite the Astoria. That was where he lived.

Herr Hennicke went into the kitchen and put the lamp on the table. He carried the large green stamp album under his arm. 'Bedtime, Meta.'

Meta smiled up from her letter, shy and embarrassed. Her blue eyes looked good-natured if gormless, and her smarmed-down hair shone yellow like wheat.

Herr Hennicke, with a sly smile, raised a finger of warning: 'A little love letter?'

'No, not at all,' smirked Meta, mournfully. 'Certainly not.' Oh, Herr Hennicke had no idea how the man messed her around. Why did she lie down with him that time in the park and let him do anything he wanted? Well, he had wanted to then, and now he'd had enough.

'Be that as it may,' said Herr Hennicke. 'You go straight to bed, all right?'

'Yes, Herr Hennicke.' And when Herr Hennicke had gone, she wrote at the bottom of the letter: 'Just leave it. I'm fed up of asking. Stay away then. You only wanted to have your fun with me by the ramparts. Now I know exactly what kind of man you are. I won't let it happen again.'

The dance was over and the couples came down off the raised dance floor back to their tables. The helmsman had danced with Berta again. 'If you carry on making eyes at that negro, you needn't come on Thursday afternoon,' he had said. 'I don't want to anyway,' Berta snapped. 'There are masses of people like you.' 'Well, have fun with your negro. He's coming after you already.' The helmsman simply left her standing in the middle of the garden, surrounded by people. The negro came up close to her, she looked into his powerful eyes, which glistened bluish-white, at his open mouth, the rough brown-blue skin with its wide pores, and sank into the accompanying encouraging smile. 'Come on,' said the negro. 'Want to?' And he made his way through the tables, under the veranda. Berta looked after the helmsman, at her husband, then followed the negro. On the back wall of the veranda was a door to the courtyard with the elm, where the pieces of scenery stood, the yard between the stage area and the wooden shacks. This was the door they went through.

The soft, dark sound of a gong rang through the garden. The announcer, who had hit the cymbal, stood on the stage. As silence fell he called out: 'Ladies and gentlemen, the wrestling continues. I hope you feel revived and ready for the next act. We have now for you the two champion wrestlers, Dieckmann and Alvaroz. These two champions have never fought each other before, they meet tonight for the first time. The hugely experienced Dieckmann, tried and tested, always the winner, and Alvaroz, the hope of things to come, the young face of victory, at the dynamic start of his career. We are proud to have been able to engage these two men, so as to offer you what will be an extraordinary fight. Mr Music. . .' The band leader went back under the canopy and the band played, blaring, staccato, the Toreador Song from *Carmen*.

The announcer leaned, arms crossed, against the wall at the edge of the stage, watching in anticipation. Two bellboys carried on a table, placing it at the back of the stage, then two chairs. They were followed by two fat, worthy-looking men in bowler hats with watch chains across their stomachs. They sat down, and one opened a briefcase and took a fountain pen out of his waistcoat pocket. These were the two umpires. Then came Hein Dieckmann, led by Jonny. He walked a little stiffly, his face like a bull. 'You've got to win,' whispered Jonny, pinching his arm. 'How do you feel?'

'Fantastic,' said Hein, darkly.

'Gather your strength,' whispered Jonny. 'You don't need me to tell you that.'

Jonny let go of him, stepped back beside the announcer and Dieckmann bowed grumpily. The audience greeted Hein with hearty applause and cheers. Some were slightly annoyed at Hein's uncivil behaviour. He's an arrogant so-and-so. Who does he think he is? Don't give yourself airs, Hein, better see how it goes, wait till you've seen the other chap. . . A couple of Alvaroz's passionate supporters even whistled.

Sluggish and stooping slightly, Hein withdrew from the footlights.

'What's the matter with him? Why's he in such a mood?' asked the announcer.

'Oh, had some kind of run-in with Alvaroz,' said Jonny.

The announcer whistled. 'Not rising to the bait?'

'No,' said Jonny. 'But wait till you see him get to work on the lad. He'll be laughing on the other side of his face.'

With a nimble leap Alvaroz appeared at the front of the stage, gallantly raised a well-formed arm and bowed. Initially the applause was not as vigorous as for Hein, but it then got stronger and stronger. The audience looked with pleasure at the taut, well-trained body, which gleamed bronze-brown, the firm, neat movements, the straight posture. Alvaroz's black hair shone like a mirror, his eyes were strong and full and his teeth flashed when he smiled. The women's eyes flitted all over his skin. They leaned forward, clapping, ecstatic.

'You must admit, he looks fantastic,' said Anton. 'The other one's fat and ugly in comparison.'

'We'll just watch this fight,' said Oskar, 'then we need to get back to the steamer.'

'Yes, all right,' said Anton, craning his neck. The fat man next to him had woken up again; he sat forward, his hat pushed back, and stared at Alvaroz: 'Good Lord, look at him. There's a Grecian, if ever I've seen one!'

'Grecian?' said Oskar. 'Italian more like, or Spanish. . .'

'Well, you know what I mean. . . Don't take it so literally.'

Alvaroz leaped back and braced himself, his calves, his firm thighs quivering like a young colt. Dieckmann cast a furtive glance at him, his face like thunder. He murmured something to himself.

The announcer had noticed Nita and Fred, standing off to one side in front of the veranda; they had pulled their summer coats on over their conspicuous costumes, but flashes of Nita's sequin dress still sparkled at the collar. Fred stared coldly at the girl, who was following Alvaroz's every move with a rapt expression.

'The old chap's sitting in the front row,' said Jonny.

The announcer looked at the manager of the Astoria. He was right, he was sitting in the front row. He only came once an evening, so the most important moment had arrived.

He was fat and puffed up, with hair that gleamed right to the nape of his neck. His oily gaze rested with absent-minded dreariness on the young wrestler, and once he managed to raise his hands in an attempt at dull applause. Then his stubby, ring-covered fingers splayed once more across his fat thigh.

I'm going to go and ask him later if I can ask him later for some time off, decided the announcer. Just a few hours and he'd be able to do so much good at home. Flowers to his wife, lock up the flat, take their son to a children's home, he could manage all that, couldn't he?

Then it was time to begin. He gave a signal for the music to stop. It broke off. 'Your attention, please,' he called. Dieckmann and Alvaroz positioned themselves facing each other, and the announcer put a little whistle to his lips and blew. 'Begin,' he called, cutting the air sharply with his arm.

And Dieckmann and Alvaroz began to spar. The band played muted music, reacting to their movements, and all was suddenly quiet in the crowd. Tentatively, the wrestlers began to slap their hands against each other's bodies, trying to find a good place to attack, then slipping away, moving forward again, brushing past, circling around noiselessly like two panthers. It was a silent game of limbs, not connecting quite yet, a brief clasp, wrapping round each other, pushing away. But they were aroused by every touch, goaded on, forced together: the friction was electric.

Alvaroz was initially the more mobile; Dieckmann still had something sluggish and brooding about him. Alvaroz slipped away from him, lunged forward again, prancing nimbly round Dieckmann, grabbed his arm and bent it back, was hurled back, fell, then up again, another lunge forward.

Then a sudden blow from Dieckmann knocked him to the floor and Dieckmann threw himself over Alvaroz, abdomen against abdomen, his mouth against Alvaroz's hairy chest, rubbing his lips for a second against the firm hairs, a steel-like grip to the upper arm laid Alvaroz on his back, Dieckmann wrapped his legs through his opponent's, stamping, panting: 'Got you at last, lad. You'll have to keep still now, eh?'

'No,' cried Alvaroz, throwing Dieckmann off to one side, seizing him by the neck, and Dieckmann grabbed hold of his neck, too, and they rolled across the floor, leaped up, rolled over again and Alvaroz sprang to his feet: free. 'Bravo,' clapped the audience. 'Give it to him, Alvaroz. Let him have it!'

Bull-necked, his head lowered, Dieckmann charged towards him. 'Fuckers,' he murmured with rage. He grabbed him by the shoulder. 'That's the last time you get away from me, lad. Now come here, my little prince.' He hooked his leg round Alvaroz's, threw him down and was on top of him again, grinning. 'Weren't expecting that, were you?' As if he suddenly had ten hands rather than two, he squeezed Alvaroz all over, holding him fast, and again his thick lips, his eyes were right up against Alvaroz's chest, up at his throat, chuckling with pleasure. 'And here we are again. Sorry, is that not what you wanted? I've got you now, lad. Don't look like that. Be a good boy now. Ooh—feel that. What a nice young lad. . .' 'Bastard!' shouted Alvaroz, his bold eyes rolling with rage.

'Such a gorgeous body, and with me on top, whether he likes it or not. Nothing he can do,' sniggered Dieckmann. Alvaroz had twisted himself to one side, but could not get loose. 'You animal,' he cursed. 'Behave yourself.'

The announcer had bent over the wrestlers. 'Dieckmann, what are you doing? Come to your senses, man.'

He blew his whistle. Dieckmann did not care any more, he was unreachable. He rolled on top of Alvaroz, laughing, talking to himself, running his lightning hands over Alvaroz's body, but when Alvaroz tried to break free he again had him in his grasp, pressing himself against him.

'Now will you be my dear little boy?' he threatened, his eyes vacant.

'You dog,' cried Alvaroz.

'Now will you be my dear little boy?'

'No!'

'Will you?'

'No!'

Fiercer and fiercer: 'Will you, will you, will you?'

'You animal!'

The umpires were leaning right over the table, one desperately ringing a little bell, the announcer blew his whistle and shouted: 'Stop!' Jonny stamped his foot hard on the wooden floor: 'Hein, Hein.' The manager had initially sat there wide-eyed, but now leaped up: 'This really is unacceptable. What is going on? This isn't a wrestling match', and ran up the wooden steps onto the stage: 'Gentlemen, stop! I will not tolerate such behaviour in my establishment. . .'

The audience rose from their seats, moved towards the footlights, screaming in indignation and staring at the stage. 'Down with Dieckmann, down with Dieckmann!'

Then all of a sudden Dieckmann reared up, his head blood-red, his vacant eyes half open, holding Alvaroz away from him, and then suddenly began pummelling Alvaroz's body with his great fists, gasping, wailing: 'You gorgeous boy, you horrible gorgeous lump, you don't want to? Take that, and that, and that, and that. . .' He punched Alvaroz in the face and blood streamed from his nose, punched him in the mouth so that his lips burst, punched his chest, wherever he could. Alvaroz tried to get up, but each time the thunderous blows knocked him back down.

Then Dieckmann lay completely on top of him, right up close, pressing his mouth against Alvaroz's bloody mouth: 'Oh, my boy, my dear, dear boy, you poor, beautiful boy.' And with that he fell, senseless, to one side, his eyes open but turned upward so that they were almost invisible, and the men standing around could finally push him to one side and set Alvaroz free. He lay groaning on the floor, his throat rattling, smeared with blood and sweat, scratched, smashed to pieces.

The audience screamed, whistled and shook their fists: 'Down with Dieckmann, down with Dieckmann! It's a disgrace!' Everyone was standing on the tables or in tight rows in front of the stage, their heads looking up at the two wrestlers. Everything was in chaos; some had already left the garden, calling the waiter for the bill.

The manager stood at the edge of the stage with a large megaphone: 'Ladies and gentlemen, do please calm yourselves—an awkward little incident, quite unexpected—do please stay—gentlemen at the back, please don't go. The stage will be cleared, and everything will soon be in order again. Music, please, something nice and jolly. Ladies and gentlemen, come and dance, please, enjoy yourselves—my sincere apologies—ladies and gentlemen, we have such a wonderful programme for you, the best acts are still to come.'

The band started up again. The manager handed the megaphone to the announcer: 'That should have been your job.' He sighed. 'It's always the way. At crucial moments one must do things oneself.' He cast a sorrowful glance at the beer garden, which had calmed down now somewhat. 'First of all, get this pair off,' he said. Nita and Fred were standing next to Alvaroz, Fred staring motionless at the battered body: 'Well, there he is, your hero,' he said quietly. Nita had forgotten to hold her coat together, it was hanging open, and her sequin dress shimmered in the lamplight. She wrinkled her nose: 'Ugh, how repulsive.'

The umpires and two bellboys carried Alvaroz off the stage. Berta saw them as they made their way through the courtyard. She was sitting on the bench under the elm with the negro.

'What's all that?' she said.

'I think he had enough,' grinned the negro, stroking her leg.

She slapped his hand. 'Stop it. I'm going. You wait here a bit.'

'That was quick.'

'Always leave them wanting more.' Berta stood up, arranging her dress and hair. 'Here comes another picture of misery.'

They could hear sharp, high-pitched whistles coming from the beer garden. 'Dieckmann,' said the negro.

Dieckmann propped himself up on Jonny and, doubled up and limp, and still hanging onto Jonny, climbed down the little wooden steps from the stage into the courtyard. He stared gloomily.

'You idiot,' said Jonny. 'What are you, possessed or something?'

'I am such a cruel bastard,' sighed Hein. 'Didn't even know myself I was that cruel.' Tears welled up in his eyes.

'It was going to happen sooner or later.'

'They didn't want any more, any of them, and I couldn't bear it,' said Hein.

'Well, you've had enough now,' said Jonny.

Hein lay down on the chaise longue in his room and stared at the ceiling.

'Cheer up,' said Jonny, and hit Hein encouragingly on the shoulder with a hefty slap. 'It's all in the past now, over.'

Hein shook his head, and his cheeks shone wet in the cold light: 'I can't believe I did something like that. Just can't believe it. . .'

People had gone back to their seats and were chatting excitedly about what had happened, the band played, but no one wanted to dance. A bellboy in a lilac uniform, his cap askew, was kneeling on the stage and washing away the blood with a cloth.

'You can't do that with a dry cloth, boy,' wailed the manager.

The boy looked up nervously at the wide trail of blood and then at the face of the manager; the hand holding the cloth was trembling.

'This really isn't a job for a little boy,' said the announcer timidly.

'Of course it is,' said the manager, shaking his head in despair. 'They need to get used to such things. Quick, get a bucket of hot water and a broom. Got it?' The boy shot off.

'Sir,' said the announcer, 'I have something to ask you.'

'A private matter?' said the manager immediately, looking at him suspiciously.

'Yes.'

'Not now, dear chap. How can you think of such things? I do wonder. Come on, get a bit of atmosphere going. It's enough to make anyone weep out here. Then come and see me in my office. I wanted to talk to you anyway.'

Oskar and Anton had paid for their beers and stood up. 'Evening,' they said to the man at their table. 'Evening,' said the man, sitting there replete with satisfaction.

As they went through the archway onto the harbour road, Anton said: 'This evening really is jinxed, first the incident with Bauer and now this.'

'I'll be jolly glad to be back in my rooms in Marburg.'

'Well, not long and you'll be in Amsterdam, with Calvin.'

'Thank God,' said Oskar.

Somewhat pale and tentative, Berta rejoined Karl at their table. 'What's been going on here?'

'Where were you the whole time?'

'Oh, I had to go out, I felt so queer, my stomach—it's all right again now.'

'They almost killed each other in here.'

'Your name's Peter, isn't it?' said Fanny. 'A right stuffy little Peter you are.' She snuggled down in the bed, pulled the covers up to her chin and put her hands behind her head. She looked at him reproachfully.

He did not look at her at all.

'You're really going to get dressed?'

'You can see I am.'

'You're going to get dressed and leave, just like that?'

Peter nodded gloomily.

'And there I was thinking today would be real nice, real different.'

'Well, it's certainly been different from usual,' said Peter.

'Yes, but I mean, real nice. I really like you.'

'I liked you, too, and I thought. . .'

'Come here, you,' said Fanny. She got up and pulled him over to the edge of the bed. She looked him in the face. 'You were so nice to me. And now you don't like me any more?'

'No, I do,' said Peter.

'And that big, red mouth of yours, too. Don't you feel like it?'

Peter looked to one side. 'I can't talk about things like that.'

'Why not? Why don't you want to carry on?'

He looked at her pointed, bony shoulders, at her button nose, turned up in incomprehension, and gave a pained smile.

'I thought it would work, but it's gone now, I don't feel anything any more.'

'Wasn't I nice to you, then?' She looked at the table. There, in the dark, still stood the bottle of liqueur and the glasses, shimmering slightly in the light from the street. 'You had a drink and listened to the gramophone. Didn't it get you in the mood?'

'Oh, the same old rubbish,' said Peter.

'You're just not a real man,' she said and went back to bed, pulling the covers up to her chin. 'Go on then, get dressed!'

He sat back down on the edge of the bed and bent down for his shoes. She came up to him from behind, pressing her breasts against his back, seizing his shoulders and over into his open shirt, stroking his chest.

'Stop it,' he said.

'Come here,' she said.

'There's no point.'

'You don't feel anything, do you? For once I've found someone I actually like, and he doesn't want to.'

'It won't work,' said Peter. 'I can't.'

'Why not?'

'Don't know.'

'Come here,' she said. 'Come here, you. There. . . Why are you so sad?. . . You silly. . .'

Stiff and grave, the inspector walked on. On one side of the street stood the white row of houses in Olbersstrasse, silent, the windows dark or with curtains drawn, on the other side ran the railway embankment. The grassy slope shone a dull green in the ghostly lamplight. Above the embankment rose the dark-green tops of the trees in the park. The inspector's footsteps rang hard and military on the pavement. Then the inspector saw the sausage-stand under the railway bridge. The sausage man in his white smock, an apron tied round, stood under the reddish glow of the paraffin lamp beside the steaming pan, chatting with two workmen who were chomping on their sausages and laughing. The inspector hesitated. The laughter echoed under the railway bridge. Otherwise the street was quite quiet, the occasional cyclist with a wobbling light went by, or the dull rumble of a car going under the bridge. Then the workmen left, and the inspector suddenly decided to march up to the sausage-stand. He could already smell the pleasing scent of frying.

'Evening, Inspector. Still out and about, enjoying the air?'

'Yes, Krömke,' said the inspector, in a strict, measured tone. His spectacles flashed.

'Quite right, too, Inspector. It's a nice time for a walk, now the air's a bit cooler.'

'Business good, Krömke?' asked the inspector.

'Yes, thank you.' Krömke let out a large, satisfied laugh, leaning on the table, one hand on the lid of the pan, and bent forward in a confidential way, his round rosy face, his short blond hair all beaming with quiet pleasure: 'Thanks very much. It's evenings like this, you see, that brings them out, everyone's out and about, they stand around in the street, chatting, they're all relaxed in the evening, you see, the busy day's over, you can enjoy yourself, breathe in the air, and they get a bit peckish and—*snap*—it pops into their head: fancy a sausage? Yes, why not? What a good idea. And then you've got the couples, of course. They go into the park first for a bit of how's your father, then they fancy something to eat and. . .'

'That's enough, Krömke. I understand,' said the inspector, looking gravely at the pan. 'I'll have two bratwursts again, please.'

'Wrapped up, to take away?'

'Of course, Krömke. As usual.'

'Inspector,' said Krömke, his violet eyes suddenly turning quite soft and wistful, 'may I ask you something?'

'Fire away, Krömke,' said the inspector, looking warily up and down the street. 'Quickly, though, Krömke. I can't chat long.'

'Inspector, why do you never eat your sausages by my stand?'

'I always take them away with me. They taste better at home. What a silly, superfluous question, Krömke.'

'Inspector,' said Krömke reproachfully, 'I know for a fact you don't eat the sausages at home. You go over into the park and eat them there.'

'All right, at home, in the park, it's doesn't matter. Good God, is a man not free to eat his sausages where he likes? Are you my wife, Krömke? Whatever has got into you, an otherwise reasonably sensible. . .'

'Oh, Inspector, I know full well why you go to the park: eating by my stand embarrasses you.'

'Nonsense,' scolded the inspector. 'Don't be silly. . .'

'No, it does, it embarrasses you. It's not refined enough for you. And I get lots of gents eat here. For example, there's Herr. . .'

'I can't listen to any more of this silly nonsense.'

'Inspector, hand on heart, am I right?'

'And if you are, Krömke,' said the inspector, 'it has nothing to do with you, it needn't offend you.'

'Well, it does offend me, it hurts me. . .'

'It needn't do, Krömke. Now don't be so childish. You need to understand life. . .'

'I do that,' said Krömke gloomily.

'You need to realise there are certain limits, certain obligations. On account of one's position, Krömke, the uniform.'

Krömke looked pensively at the inspector's green jacket, gold buttons and sparkling epaulettes. 'Yes, limits everywhere,' he said quietly. 'And to what end?'

'One cannot be too careful,' said the inspector. 'Enemies, a nasty rumour—if only everyone was like you, Krömke. . .'

Nodding sympathetically, in silence, Krömke laid two pale-pink sausages on the grill, turning them back and forth with a fork as they browned and crackled in the fat.

'No, I've nothing against your occupation,' said the inspector. 'Nothing whatsoever. A perfectly decent, respectable trade. And not easy, it can't be easy. . .'

'In the winter particularly,' added Herr Krömke with a modest, suffering air. 'In the cold. It's all right at this time of year.'

'I'm sure it's not that easy now either,' said the inspector. 'But you have my thanks, standing up for hours on end at your table.'

'It's possible to sit down, too,' said Krömke.

'Nevertheless, nevertheless, hats off to you.'

Krömke laid the brown sausages, glistening with fat, on a paper plate, together with a good dollop of mustard and a bread roll, wrapped it all carefully in a paper napkin and handed it to the inspector: 'Well, Inspector, there are your sausages. Off you go to the park now, if you must—*bon appétit*—and no hard feelings.'

'Good evening, Krömke. You are an understanding man. I take my hat off to you.'

'Good evening, Inspector,' said Krömke and, with heavy heart, he watched him gravely walk away. The inspector's footsteps echoed under the railway bridge, and his epaulettes sparkled in the lamplight. He carried his parcel in front of him, stiff and solemn. Krömke saw him plunge into the park.

Little Luise was asleep again, she had been woken by a dream but she had forgotten that dream again now and had sunk into sleep. But her mother could still not sleep. She lay with her in the same room, she had gone to the window, had thought of her dead husband, who had lain buried in St Peter's churchyard for two years, and she had gone back to bed, now she lay there, her eyes open. She thought about Luise and her dreams, she thought about her husband and their other daughter, Anni, who had married the art teacher. She did not sleep with them any more, she had freed herself from them, and now lay beside a man. Did Anni like it, would she manage? She said so little about it.

Oh, at that moment Anni was not happy, she was anxious and worried, for she was alone, Georg had not come back from the bowling night with his teaching colleagues and she too was lying there with her eyes open, tossing and turning and waiting. . .

She had finally just nodded off to sleep when she was woken by a jangle of keys. Georg! How loud he was, slamming the door, stamping along the corridor. Was it Georg?

The door opened wide, a figure stood in the doorway. She heard quiet laughter.

'Georg, turn the light on!' called Anni.

The figure stood there, laughing.

Anni switched on the bedside lamp with trembling hands. It was Georg. 'You gave me a fright. Georg, Georg—you're drunk—oh God, he's drunk.'

With great ceremony, using both hands, Georg closed the door and stumbled into the room, held onto the headboard of Anni's bed and leaned over with a stupid grin: 'It was good fun,' he slurred. 'They're a good crowd, that lot. And what's my little dove been up to? Time for bed now, is it? Ha, ha. . .'

'Georg, stop it. You're really drunk. Georg, listen to me, be sensible.'

But Georg was not listening, he carried on chortling, belched loudly and raised a finger, was going to say something, could not get it out, staggered over to the mirror on the wardrobe, held himself steady and stared at his face.

'Evening,' he said, bowing to his reflection. 'What are you, what are you, what are you doing here, eh? With my wife?'

'If you're going to be like this, then I won't be your wife,' shouted Anni. She lay stiff in bed, she had sat up slightly and pulled the covers up to her head. What had happened to Georg's kind face, his calm, friendly manner? If he touched her she would scream. Should she simply run away, run away outside? She was alone, completely alone, abandoned with this strange man, in a strange house, in the night. . .

Then Georg caught sight of Anni's horrified face in the mirror, the terror-stricken eyes, her lip curled up in disgust, black hair framing a white face. He saw her delicate little hands, trembling as they snatched up the covers. And he turned round. He drew himself up and walked over to the bed with his normal step, smiling in a calm, rational way, slightly embarrassed:

'It was only a joke. I was just pretending.'

Anni stared at him for a short while, examining, then her face relaxed, twitched, smiled timidly, and then she cried, sank back and cried, broken, happy, shaken.

'Oh, you mustn't do that. It wasn't nice.'

Georg sat on the edge of the bed and looked at her, embarrassed. 'I was just having a joke. Didn't you think it was funny?'

'No, I did not think it was funny. Oh, I was really scared. I was so alone all of a sudden. It wasn't you. There was a strange man in the room.'

'But I'm back again now. Look at me. I'm completely sober. I hardly drank a thing.' He gently stroked her hair.

Again, Anni examined his face.

'I thought it was all over.'

'Silly,' said Georg.

They looked at each other for a long time. Anni's face became bright and clear. She smiled. Georg smiled again.

'I can't believe you can change like that,' she said, shaking her head slightly. 'You must never do it again.' A breeze came through the open window, light and soft, gently blowing the white curtains.

'No,' he said. He sat peacefully on her bed, and they looked at each other and recognised each other again, completely.

The inspector sat on the bench. He had eaten his two sausages in the darkness of the park, biting into the hot, spicy meat with a certain greediness and appeasing the hunger he always felt late at night. He leaned back, looking over the grassy embankment at the water, and saw the water lilies, shimmering soft and indistinct, the black, motionless surface of the pond, the sleeping swans. He stretched, he savoured the air, he felt like he was floating in the thick atmosphere, gently dissolving into it, his spectacles slid from his nose and he began to doze off.

A train thundered over the railway bridge, over Herr Krömke's head, and went rattling along the embankment, past the ramparts, past the dull-white row of houses in Olbersstrasse. The inspector woke with a start. He saw the lights of the train flying through the black water, coursing over the swans, the bushes and trees. He pulled himself together. It was high time he went to bed. Otherwise he would be of no use at work first thing tomorrow morning. He stood up and walked away with measured steps.

He went out of the park and under the railway bridge, Herr Krömke waving a friendly 'Good night' from the other side.

'Good night,' and he went on to the harbour road. There was still noise and light from certain restaurants on the other side—a door opened and the plink-plonk of an electric piano floated out into the empty street—on the other side, however, the wine-red customs house lay silent, its windows dark. And the inspector crossed the street, towards his front door. He stood at the door, lifting up his green jacket so he could pull out the heavy, impressive bunch of keys from his trouser pocket when he heard a shrill, woeful cry and men's voices cursing, nearby. He looked up and turned round.

A small boy in a white sailor suit was running in great haste along the other side of the road, past the large illuminated or shuttered windows of the restaurants, he had his little fists clenched to his chest, running as fast as he could and crying all the while. A tiny dachshund hopped along beside him, occasionally leaping up with a joyful whine. And not far behind them ran a large, solid man in a black tailcoat which streamed out behind him, evidently trying to catch the little boy. And a short distance after that another man came running, trying to catch up with the large man. It was Addi and Fips and the hypnotist and the announcer, running along the harbour road.

The hypnotist finally caught up with Addi, tore him round by the shoulder, put his other hand on his other shoulder and shook the boy, making his delicate little blond head fly back and forth like a bud of a flower on a feeble stem: 'Where are you off to, eh? What are doing running around the streets at night, on your own, without my say-so? Doing a bunk, I suppose? Answer me.'

'No,' breathed Addi.

'What did you run off for? What is all this nonsense?'

'I wasn't running away, honest,' sobbed Addi.

The announcer had caught up with them. 'Leave the poor boy in peace,' he said. 'You've tormented him enough today as it is.'

'What are you doing here?' asked the hypnotist. 'A fine thing if I can't make my boy see sense. The scamp was trying to do a bunk, I can see that. I'm not blind.'

He gave Addi a resounding slap round the head and then seized him by the ears and hauled his head back and forth. 'Were you doing a bunk? Well? Tell me.'

'No, no, no,' screamed Addi.

At that moment the grave steps of the inspector crossed the street and approached the hypnotist. He fended him off with his hand: 'Please, let go of that child. You can't discipline him like that.' The hypnotist saw the inspector's firm stare, he saw the green uniform and the disapproving look of authority, and he let Addi go.

'Ah, lieutenant, let me explain: the little urchin was doing a bunk.'

'Is it any wonder the boy can't bear being with you? You torture him to the quick,' said the announcer. 'Lieutenant,' he said to the inspector, 'this is the hypnotist from the Astoria. He puts on performances there with his son which run the boy into the ground.'

The hypnotist forced a short laugh.

'Listen, you impudent lout. What's it got to do with you? Some colleague you are.'

'The act should be banned,' said the announcer. 'Lieutenant, couldn't you do something? The police just can't allow children to be tortured like that.'

'I'm not a police lieutenant. I'm a customs inspector,' said the inspector, clearing his throat. He ran his finger round his high, stiff collar in embarrassment. 'You'll have to find someone else.'

'Barking up the wrong tree,' laughed the hypnotist. 'Well, go on, you philanthropist, run to the police and pour your heart out. Won't do you much good.' The hypnotist stood before the announcer, legs apart, arms folded, his healthy, red-cheeked face beaming in triumph. Infinitesimally small, Addi stood next to his father and stared with a hopeless, weary look at the window of Meyer's fishmongers, in front of which they were standing. The shop was in darkness, but in the window was a fish tank which was lit from beneath; the water glowed green, a pipe bubbled in on one side, and a couple of fat fish were floating silently in the water, asleep, while others were still swimming anxiously back and forth, flinging about their oily, silver-scaled bodies and staring blearily at the street, at Addi. The little dachshund had sat down on the pavement in front of Addi, watching him and the big men with a furrowed brow and bright, clever eyes.

'Have you no feeling for the boy? Can't you see his health's failing?' asked the announcer meekly.

'Nonsense,' said the hypnotist.

'But he was sick again only today. I saw it.'

'Only because of that stupid incident with the mutt. He's had it. Yes, you filthy creature, don't look like that. And wagging your tail won't do anything.'

Addi began to cry again, quietly. Helpless, he gazed at the inspector. The inspector turned away smartly. He rubbed his chin in thought. Addi looked again at the fish, which stared, goggle-eyed, through the glass.

'The child shouldn't be allowed to stay with you,' said the announcer in despair. 'He needs to be taken away. You're no father. Sir,' he said to the inspector, 'you've seen yourself how he treats the child. You could testify if needs be. Can't we find him somewhere else to stay? Find a decent person to take him in and look after him properly?'

The hypnotist stood there motionless, laughing a little to himself. Addi looked expectantly at the announcer, and for a few seconds there was a small glimmer of amazement in his eyes. The inspector raised his head, stepped a little closer in his stiff, ungainly way and his old, grey eyes flashed behind his spectacles, he cleared his throat, tried to say something, but then he saw the hypnotist, standing there quite imperturbable and laughing to himself, so he looked away with a shy, embarrassed smile and said: 'A question, if I may: can children as young as this be used, legally, for the purposes of entertainment? I mean. . .'

'No, of course they can't!' cried the announcer. 'But thank you for saying it, sir. The police will soon put a stop to all this. I hope so, at least.'

'You can hope all you like,' said the hypnotist. He whisked out a fat pocketbook and rooted around in it. 'Here we are. The permit.'

'Inconceivable,' murmured the inspector.

'Inconceivable to you, who knows nothing about these matters. You see? I'm completely within my rights. And if you bleat on much longer I shall go to the police and file an action against you. Right, that's an end to it. I've had enough of this twaddle. Next time, think a bit harder before you go disturbing an honest man in his work, which is difficult enough as it is. Good night, gentlemen. I hope you sleep well and will have seen sense by the morning.' He turned to the announcer: 'I've got another bone to pick with you. But not here. Addi, hand.'

Addi's head sank forward again and he meekly raised his hand, his father seized it firmly and they departed. The dachshund pattered along behind them, ears swinging. The hypnotist's footsteps rang out along the silent street.

'Now he's got him again. It's dreadful,' said the announcer.

'Can nothing be done?' asked the inspector.

'I don't know,' said the announcer wearily. 'Now even the law is on his side.'

'Do you know what?' said the inspector, with a bashful laugh. 'When you first asked if there was anyone who might. . .'

'I knew it!' cried the announcer. 'Why didn't you say something?'

'There was no point.'

'Of course there was,' said the announcer. 'You don't have any family, I take it?'

'No, not at all.'

'Such a shame, such a shame. I would have let you have him. He's a such good boy.'

'Yes, my wife is dead, and I don't have any children.'

'Sorry, but I need to get back,' said the announcer.

'Is it worth trying the police?'

'Maybe, but I don't hold out much hope. I've got too much on my plate at the moment. My wife's ill. I need to visit her.'

'Oh,' said the inspector.

They shook hands and, dejected, the announcer walked slowly back to the Astoria. The inspector opened his front door and, stiff and grave, climbed the dark stairs to his lonely flat.

A couple of waiters and bellboys ran up to the announcer as soon as he reached the Astoria: 'Where have you been? We've been looking everywhere. . .'

'Well, calm yourselves, I'm here now,' said the announcer, and walked through the beer garden into the rear courtyard, where the elm tree and pieces of scenery stood. A man and a girl, who were dressed as trappers, came up to him in great excitement: 'There you are. Everything's a mess. Where have you been?' The man and the girl were wearing brown leather costumes, with red bandanas round their necks and large hats on their heads. They shook their heads angrily and the large rings in their ears waggled.

'Quick, on the stage,' cried the trapper, his eyes fervent.

A bellboy leaped up to the announcer. 'You've got to go straight to the manager,' he said in a bright, child's voice.

'All right,' said the announcer. 'I'm coming.'

'No, go on stage first, to announce us,' cried the trapper.

'I can do that too,' said the announcer.

He climbed onto the stage from behind, said something, almost without thinking about what it was, climbed back down and the trappers went on. A drum roll came from the band.

The announcer slowly walked into the Astoria itself, clomped up the stairs and knocked on the manager's door. When he went in it was just as he thought. The hypnotist was already there.

The manager, sitting at his desk, turned round in his chair, his fat hand splayed out on the surface of the desk. The hypnotist leaned on the edge of the desk, his arms folded, and looked at the announcer, sure of victory.

Good God, thought the announcer, take what you want. Just leave me in peace.

The manager fixed an oily, melancholy stare on the announcer: 'What are all these stories I've been hearing,

115

dear chap? This really won't do. You run off, throwing the whole operation into disarray, stick your nose into matters which are none of your business. . .'

'I couldn't watch him torturing the boy any longer,' said the announcer.

'But he wasn't tortured. That simply isn't true,' cried the manager. 'You evidently have no idea what child-rearing, what true discipline means. It's the only way to make something of children. This is a case in point. A spectacular act, the high point of our programme.'

'Well, I shan't say any more,' said the announcer.

'He's climbing down now,' laughed the hypnotist.

'My dear chap, I don't like all this,' said the manager. 'You show little interest in the business and next to no *esprit de corps* with respect to your colleagues. One simply cannot work like this. I've been watching you for some time: you bring no atmosphere to the place. What you do do has no dash. I'm sure you realise I cannot have defeatists.'

'But I've always done my duty,' said the announcer, uncertainty in his voice. He stood there, slouched, with an expressionless, grey face. Oh, they were right, he was falling apart.

'Duty,' cried the manager.

'Duty, as if that were enough,' the hypnotist chipped in.

'Quite right,' said the manager. 'Duty does not suffice. There must be something else. Do you not see that? Energy, animation, a certain originality. . .'

'I can't always be in the mood, with all my worries,' said the announcer.

'What worries?'

'My wife is very ill.'

'Well, that is provoking, but still—one must face up to such things. You walk around with that funereal expression—that just won't do. Oh, and you had something to ask me, didn't you say?'

'Oh, it's nothing important.'

'Come on, out with it!'

'Oh, I wanted to ask for a day's leave, so that I could go and visit my wife.'

'I thought as much,' moaned the manager. 'The job always comes second with you. Your mind is constantly elsewhere. No, no: there's no point.' Heaving a sigh, the manager got up and went over to the announcer, held him by the arm with his fleshy hand and gave him a sad, oily look: 'My dear chap, as much as it pains me, I think we should part company. You don't fit in with my establishment. I expected a lot from you: announcers who can also do wrestling are rare, but if you do it in such a dull, pedestrian way then I cannot set great store by such prerogatives. I was wrong about you. You can work for another day or two, until a replacement is found, and then you can go. Agreed?'

'Yes,' said the announcer. 'All right.'

'Of course it's all right, dear chap,' said the manager, giving him an encouraging nudge. 'Don't take it too much to heart. These things are sent to try us. You can visit your wife now. That was what you wanted.'

The announcer stood there, speechless, and looked at the floor. Then he slowly turned towards the door and left the room. He went down the stairs and out into the garden, the trapper act was already over and people were dancing. He walked through the veranda into the rear courtyard and sat on the bench under the elm. He stared at the scenery depicting Stolzenfels Castle on the Rhine. To one side stood two wrestlers, chatting. The hypnotist came into the yard, in his mouth a fat cigar the manager had given him, he looked at the announcer and walked behind him past the elm, up to the wrestlers. They were talking about Alvaroz. 'What, didn't you see him? You should go look. He's still lying there.' Yes, they'd come. They knew which dressing room was his. They went into the wooden shack and Alvaroz's room. Switched on the light. Alvaroz was still asleep. One of the wrestlers gently pulled back the robe they had laid over him. The hypnotist looked at the battered body. Alvaroz had not yet been cleaned up, and blood clung red-black to his body. Bluish patches, tinged with mother-of-pearl, had appeared on his skin. These were where Dieckmann's fists had hit him. His lips had burst and now gaped, and his black, slicked-down hair was ruined and now hung in clumps across his forehead. His dark-blue trunks lay in tatters round his hips.

'Such a fantastic body,' said the hypnotist. 'You can see that in spite of all the wounds and the blood.'

'You can understand why he made Dieckmann mad. But he won't let anyone near him,' said one of the wrestlers.

'You'd have more chance with a nun,' said the other.

Suddenly, Alvaroz opened his eyes. He looked at them for a long time. Then he realised where he was and saw he was completely naked.

'What are you doing here?' he asked, looking at them angrily with his powerful eyes. He ran his hand over his blood-encrusted body.

'We were just going,' muttered the others and quickly disappeared.

Hein Dieckmann had got dressed and was leaving the

shack with Jonny. They crossed the courtyard, where the announcer, downcast, was sitting under the elm. 'Let's not go through the garden,' said Jonny. 'We can get out this way.' A gate from the yard led into an alleyway from which they came out onto the harbour road. Hein wore a short, yellow coat and a bowler hat on his round head. He stared straight ahead and said nothing. Jonny shot him the occasional sidelong glance. If he said something, Hein just nodded absently. They walked along the harbour road, they were staying further into the town, in a hotel. They went past the moat. Hein stopped for a moment, took a deep breath and looked at the black water.

'Shall I tell you something?' began Jonny.

'Hm?'

'Forget the whole thing, and tomorrow you start a completely new life.'

'Bosh.'

'Now you know what you have to watch out for,' said Jonny.

'What difference will that make, you ass?'

'It'll work if you want it to,' said Jonny.

'Bah, it goes too deep,' said Hein and looked at the murky black water. 'It's in my whole body. There's nothing I can do. I'm a bastard, and that's that.'

Jonny sniffed, embarrassed and irritated. 'I almost think you're putting it on. Pull yourself together, man.'

'I'm just horrible,' said Hein. 'I'm a piece of shit, and that's that.'

Herr Berg's flute got quieter and quieter. The final crystal-clear notes breathed across the garden, blown by the wind, melting in the still air—and the music stopped. Herr Berg had finished. He lowered the flute from his lips and stood by the window a while longer, looking out into the night. Then he went back into the dark parlour.

'He's finally stopped playing,' said Frau Jacobi.

'Yes, finally,' sighed Frau Mahler. 'These young folk, they don't realise how serious life can be.'

'I don't know about that,' said Frau Jacobi. 'He's at death's door.'

The two women were sitting at the table with the electric lamp, which cast a warm, red light around the room. Frau Mahler sat on the sofa, her eyes swollen from crying, her hands in her lap, and in one hand she held a handkerchief, screwed up into a little ball and wet with tears. Her eyes were on Frau Jacobi, who was embroidering a tablecloth. The pattern was marked out on the cloth in blue ink, and Frau Jacobi was sewing over the pattern with various different-coloured silk threads.

'I'm so grateful to have you with me at this hour,' said Frau Mahler. On the table lay a small slip of paper and a pencil. Frau Jacobi had already composed the obituary notice. From time to time Frau Mahler looked uneasily towards the half-open door which led to the room where the dead man lay. A slightly sinister blackness came through the narrow gap into the quiet room.

'I enjoy being a help to you, dear,' said Frau Jacobi. 'Leave everything to me. Tomorrow morning I'll go straight to the newspaper and hand in the death notice, and then I'll go to Cypress Undertakers. You'll be happy with Cypress. They were excellent with me. Oh, it occurs to me: did your husband want to be cremated, or a coffin?'

'I've no idea,' said Frau Mahler. 'He never spoke about it. What should I do?'

'My husband was cremated,' said Frau Jacobi. 'He thought it was cleaner. Though it's a matter of taste, of course.'

'God, what should I do?' said Frau Mahler.

'Think it over, dear. There's still time.'

The window was open, and they could hear the dull blast of a steamer's horn in the harbour, sounding out across the town.

'A steamer's leaving,' said Frau Jacobi.

The dull, plaintive sound seemed to bring it all back to Frau Mahler. She suddenly began to cry again.

'Oh, it's awful,' she said. 'I can't believe I'm alone now.'

Frau Jacobi sighed dolefully, but carried on sewing her tablecloth. She had to make sure she got the tiny green leaf exactly right, and it wasn't easy.

'Please, will you stay with me all night?' sobbed Frau Mahler.

'Yes, yes, I'll stay,' said Frau Jacobi. 'I've got to get this tablecloth finished.'

The steamer which had sounded was the *Adelaide*. The ropes had been untied, and she sailed out of the harbour, pumping slowly down the river.

Anton was up on deck, watching them leave. Oskar had stood beside him for a while, but had then gone down to the cabin; he was tired and wanted to lie down. It had been a stressful day.

Anton looked back at the town. The lights edged closer and closer together, finally merging into a dull glow, a long yellow streak, and then the streak was swallowed up too, dissolved, and they sailed through the dark countryside.

The flat meadows passed swiftly by. Houses lay in black clumps by the dyke, gliding past, gantries in the dockyards rose into the night and were gone. And for a few moments, in the cloudy sky, the moon showed its old grey, silvery face, casting a sheen on the water and a dull, grey gleam over the endless fields, in which motionless animals stood or lay in the thick grass, dark, heavy shapes.

And on they went. The river became wider and wider, while the number of houses on the shore dwindled. The air gradually turned fresher and a cool breeze began to blow—a sea breeze.

Anton remained standing on deck and looked out into space.

Then all of a sudden someone was standing next to him, a figure had silently appeared. It was Bauer, the steward.

'What, are you still here? Didn't you leave?' cried Anton in surprise.

'I know, you can give me a good talking to,' said Bauer in shame. 'You're quite right.'

'Why didn't you leave?' asked Anton.

'I wanted to,' said Bauer. 'I had my things all packed. But then I couldn't. It all seemed so hopeless.'

'I would have gone anyway, if it were me,' said Anton.

'It wouldn't make any difference,' said Bauer, looking gloomily into the river. 'Stay here, go somewhere else—nothing would change.'

'Oh, I don't know,' said Anton.

'Let it go. It's just how it is,' said Bauer.

'It's insane,' said Anton.

'I'm past saving,' said Bauer.

'Herr Bauer, you mustn't talk like that. It's not true.'

'Well,' shrugged Bauer.

Then they both fell silent and looked out into the countryside.

'I should go,' said Bauer. 'Hear that? He's calling me.'

'Don't go,' advised Anton.

'No, I have to,' said Bauer. 'What else can I do?'

'It's ghastly,' said Anton.

'It is,' said Bauer, and slipped silently down the stairs from the deck.

Anton stared out into the distance with trepidation.

The steamer sailed on down the river, its dull engines pumping.

Author	Title	Foreword

AUTOBIOGRAPHY & BIOGRAPHY

Albinati, Edoardo	Coming Back	
Aubrey, John	Lives of Eminent Men	Ruth Scurr
Aubrey, John	Scientific Lives	Ruth Scurr
Brooke, Rupert	Letters from America	Benjamin Markovits
Garibaldi, Giuseppe	My Life	Tim Parks
Machiavelli, Nicolò	Life of Castruccio Castracani	Richard Overy
Mann, Klaus	Alexander	Jean Cocteau
Northup, Solomon	12 Years a Slave	
Stendhal	Letters to Pauline	Adam Thirlwell
Tagore, Rabindranath	Boyhood Days	Amartya Sen
Voltaire	Memoirs of the life of Monsieur de Voltaire	Ruth Scurr
Waiblinger, Wilhelm	Friedrich Hölderlin's Life, Poetry and Madness	
Woolf, Virginia	Platform of Time, The	

FOOD & DRINK

Bradley, Alice	Candy Cookbook, The	
Thomas, Jerry	How to Mix Drinks: Or The Bon Vivant's Companion	

HISTORY & REFERENCE

Aldrich, Mildred	Hilltop on the Marne, A	
Evans, Edward Payson	Animal Trials	
Grose, Francis	Dictionary of the Vulgar Tongue, The	
Hartley, Cecil B.	Gentlemen's Book of Etiquette, and Manual of Politeness, The	
Hartley, Florence	Ladies Book of Etiquette, and Manual of Politeness, The	
Mayhew, Henry	Wayward Genius of Henry Mayhew, The: Pioneering Reportage from Victorian London	
Wharton, Edith	Fighting France: from Dunkerque to Belfort	Colm Tóibín

LITERARY/CULTURAL STUDIES & ESSAYS

da Vinci, Leonardo	Prophecies	Eraldo Affinati
Lamb, Charles	Essays of Elia	Matthew Sweet
Margolyes, Miriam; Fraser, Sonia	Dickens' Women	
Poe, Edgar Allan	Eureka	Sir Patrick Moore
Stendhal	Memoirs of an Egotist	Doris Lessing
Swift, Jonathan	Directions to Servants	Colm Tóibín
Swift, Jonathan	Polite Conversation	Toby Litt
Tyler, Daniel	Guide to Dickens' London, A	
Woolf, Virginia	Hyde Park Gate News	Hermione Lee
Woolf, Virginia	Carlyle's House and Other Sketches	Doris Lessing
Wren, Jenny	Lazy Thoughts of a Lazy Girl	Jenny Éclair

POLITICS

Swisher, Clayton E.	Palestine Papers: The End of The Road?
Kushner, Barry	Who Needs the Cuts? Myths of
& Saville	the Economic Crisis

TRAVEL WRITING

Collins, Wilkie; Dickens, Charles	Lazy Tour of Two Idle Apprentices, The	
Fitzgerald, F. Scott	Cruise of the Rolling Junk, The	Paul Theroux
Levi, Carlo	Essays on India	Anita Desai
Levi, Carlo	Words are Stones	Anita Desai
Mayakovsky, Vladimir	My Discovery of America	Colum McCann
Miller, Henry	Aller Retour New York	